DOCTOR WHO
FRONTIOS

DOCTOR WHO
FRONTIOS

Based on the BBC television serial by Christopher H. Bidmead by arrangement with the British Broadcasting Corporation

Christopher H. Bidmead

Number 91 in the
Doctor Who Library

TARGET

A TARGET BOOK
published by
the Paperback Division of
W. H. ALLEN & Co. PLC

A Target Book
Published in 1985
by the Paperback Division of
W. H. Allen & Co. PLC
44 Hill Street, London W1X 8LB

First published in Great Britain by
W. H. Allen & Co. PLC, 1984

The BBC producer of *Frontios*
was John Nathan-Turner,
the director was Ron Jones.

Printed and bound in Great Britain by
Anchor Brendon Limited, Tiptree, Essex

ISBN 0 426 19780 1

To Alan and Marcus and
the machine that made this possible.
I'll miss their company.

Contents

1

Refugees of Mankind

At a sign from Captain Revere the diggers put up their picks and stood as still as the shadows on the chill rock walls. He said nothing as he knelt to collect more of the rock samples; he had been silent for days now, leaving it to Brazen, his second in command, to give the few necessary orders. Under the acid green light of his phosphor lamp he turned one of the small chippings in his hand, staring into its cloudy translucency with the narrowed eyes of a sailor seeking land on a far horizon.

No one knew exactly what the Captain was looking for: none of the hand-selected team of Orderlies, who now made their way back along the tunnel, their picks shouldered. Even Brazen did not know, although he always peered respectfully at the choicer samples the Captain handed to him. Precious minerals, it was said; but whether jewels, or rare metals, the Captain had not found them yet.

The clanking of a bucket above their heads heralded the return of the block and tackle. Brazen signalled to his men to load up the samples, and watched with satisfaction as the task force he had drilled sprang into action without a murmur. Not a bad improvisation, considering the resources at his disposal. Their uniforms, though well-cared-for, were patched and much-used, and the safety helmets that wrapped dark folds of metal about their faces had not been designed for this heavy work below ground, but for the weightless perils of space.

The Captain did not look up as the bucket rose and fell. He was studying the ground closely, smoothing away the surface debris. Beneath it was a strange honeycombing of the rock he had not noticed before.

Brazen heard it first and turned from the bucket with a surprising speed for a man of his build. The squeal of twisting metal meant only one thing: the shoring material was caving in under the weight of rock. He shouted to the Captain to get clear, throwing all his weight against the bulging plate-work. But the Captain lent his own lean shoulders to the work, and for the first time for days barked an order. 'Clear the area.' Lives were precious on Frontios. These few Orderlies were the planet's future.

But the plate had already cracked. Through the wound burst a spillage of debris, dark as blood. Before Brazen realised it was out of control the plate had split from top to bottom with a sound like gunshot, hurling him across the cave.

From the hole in the roof the Orderlies stared down through the swirls of dust, frozen in terror. As it settled they saw Brazen hauling himself to his feet where he had been thrown clear of rockfall. The Captain had not been so lucky. Pinioned under the collapsed props, with only his head and one shoulder visible, their leader seemed barely alive.

Swift hands pulled at the ropes. Brazen bent down over his leader, whose lips were shaping soundless words. A thick river of blood was seeping from under the fractured plate, trickling away into the strange new worm-holes in the rock.

Brazen leaped up and caught the block and tackle as it came within his reach. The movement shook the uncertain rocks into another dangerous slide, and when he looked back to guide the hook down to its destination there was no sign of Captain Revere.

Brazen engaged the hook under the heavy half-section of

plate, and waved an urgent hand to the men on the ropes. But as the block and tackle creaked under its load, where the Captain had been, Brazen was horrified to see nothing but the dark cubes of rock.

A more objective eye than his would have noticed the honey-combing of the rock floor, more extensive now, and seen perhaps in that uneven ground the faint indentation of the Captain's shape.

Brazen turned to look up at the ring of faces above him. 'I want no mention of this to anyone. You understand? To anyone!'

Turlough was no fun. He had taken to sitting on the floor beside the hat-stand, practising tying particularly tight and vicious knots in one of the Doctor's old scarves. Tegan knew what was worrying him. Since their last port of call the Doctor had become mysteriously reclusive, pottering about the corridors moving things from A to B and calling it 'getting organised'.

'It's nothing to worry about,' said Tegan. 'He . . . gets like this sometimes. He's unwinding.'

'Who's worried?' Turlough shrugged, tugging at the scarf. 'It's none of my business.'

A little later the Doctor popped his head round the door. 'Not hat people, are you, either of you? Wear them much, I mean? No, I suppose not.' He wandered over to the hat-stand. 'I only do when I go out. Silly to have this getting in everybody's way.' He was speaking to no one in particular, and Turlough did not deign to look up from his knotty problem – not, at least, until the Doctor suddenly whisked the hat-stand away and began moving towards the door with it.

'What on earth . . .!' exclaimed Turlough. But the Doctor had already swept out with a muttered 'Must get organised'.

Turlough stood up. 'That man definitely needs another

adventure. And quick. Except you can't tell him anything.'

That was true enough, Tegan reflected. Not that he wasn't always ready to help other people when the need arose, Tegan had to admit. And that gave her an idea. She shut the handbook she was reading (it was useless anyway: it kept saying '*Refer to appendix F*', and the appendices only went up to D), and, with a quick word to Turlough to stay where he was, hurried out after the Doctor.

The hat-stand with its drapery of colourful scarves and hats was disappearing down the corridor. The Doctor stopped when she called, his brow furrowed in thought. 'There's another hat-stand somewhere in the corridors. If we put the two of them side by side . . . we'll have a pair.'

Tegan brushed these important speculations aside with a shake of her neatly cropped head. 'Doctor, it's Turlough . . .'

'What's he done now?'

'Nothing. That's the problem.' She tried to make her voice sound suitably troubled, which only emphasised the twang of the Australian vowels. 'He's getting to be unbearable.' Hanging from the hat-stand was the latest victim of Turlough's handicraft, which now looked more like a string of woollen bobbles than a scarf. 'Just look at this.'

The Doctor hadn't noticed the knots. 'Hmmm . . . Good job no one was wearing it at the time.'

'He's at the end of his tether,' Tegan exaggerated. 'What he needs is an adventure.'

'There's a time for adventure and a time, Tegan, for some thorough relaxation,' the Doctor said irritably. He had begun trying to untie one of the knots, which stubbornly refused to yield. 'Turlough should realise . . . it's a chance for a gentle unwinding.' The knot seemed to give a little – or perhaps it was just the wool stretching under the strain – and the Doctor gritted his teeth and pulled harder. 'A letting go . . . A disentangling of the . . . disentangling of the . . .' His knuckles were white around the knot now, and Tegan, watching fascinated, was beginning to wonder what would give first: the knot, the scarf or the Doctor's temper.

But his mounting frustration was interrupted by the voice of Turlough shouting down the corridor. 'Doctor! Tegan! Something very funny's happening to the controls.'

They ran back to the console room. The flashing message on the small green screen said 'BOUNDARY ERROR: TIME PARAMETERS EXCEEDED'. The Doctor stared gravely at the warning. 'We've neglected things. If we don't put a stop to this, the Vortex will.'

Tegan ran through a quick co-ordinate check at the console. Beside her Turlough was interrogating the data bank. 'We've entered the Veruna System, wherever that is.' The Doctor did some swift mental arithmetic, which involved much finger-counting and tapping of his thumb against his teeth. Turlough turned to Tegan. 'How can the Vortex stop us? I thought it was what the TARDIS travelled through.'

The Doctor joined them at the console. 'We must be on the outer limits,' he said, looking fiercely at the data base screen as though that were the cause of all the trouble. 'The TARDIS has drifted far too far into the future.' And then as an afterthought he added, 'Veruna? Well, that's irony for you. It's the system where some of the last refugees of Mankind took shelter when the great . . .' The Doctor tailed off. 'Well, of course you've got all that to look forward to.'

'When the great what, Doctor?' Tegan persisted.

He waved his arms, as if some fly in the vicinity were the source of his sudden discomfiture. 'Nothing to worry about. Civilisations have their ups and downs.'

Turlough found Veruna in the data bank. ' ". . . Fleeing from the imminence of a catastrophic collision with the Sun, refugees from the doomed planet Earth set off towards the remote reaches of the Veruna System. The tiny settlements they tried to establish . . ." '

Tegan turned on the Doctor. ' "Ups and downs", you said! The data bank says "imminent catastrophe"!'

'Imminent's a relative term,' shrugged the Doctor. 'This is

all thousands of years in your future.' It wasn't easy to retain your historical perspective from the inside of a time-machine like the TARDIS. Tegan was poor Time Lord material – she was far too likely to get emotionally involved. But for Turlough, who was not born on the planet Earth, the prospect of Frontios was a lot more straightforward. He strode across the console room for a better look at the viewer screen, excitement lighting up his pale blue eyes. In front of him the shimmering rectangle depicted a small planet on which the outlines of a settlement were slowly becoming visible.

'The last humans!' he exclaimed on the edge of his breath. 'Doctor, can we land? Visit them?'

The Doctor's voice sank to a new note of gravity. 'We can't interfere. The colony's too new, one generation at the most. Its future hangs in the balance.'

Beside the small, grey-bearded man with spectacles, Brazen loomed as a huge, granite figure. So far he had tried, within the protocol of politeness to a civilian, to ignore Mr Range and his objections, but the irritation of his presence had now continued too long.

Around them, laboratory equipment was being packed into boxes. 'There is no requirement for an investigation,' Brazen barked. 'Enough said, I think, Mr Range.' He signalled to two men unbolting fittings from the wall, and they jumped down from their perch on the workbench and helped the group tying back the block and tackle.

Like a pigeon looking for the best foothold on a statue, Mr Range continued to flutter. 'There is enough distrust already of the Long Path back to knowledge. We must counter these rumours with a precise report on the tragedy . . .' The block and tackle was suspended from a sliding runner on an overhead beam traversing the room, and Mr Range had to step swiftly out of the way as it slid past him. 'Chief Orderly Brazen, I promised the colonists at the Captain's funeral I would investigate the accident.'

'You overreached yourself there, Mr Range,' snapped Brazen. 'Suffice it to know a distillation vessel exploded here in the research room.' That had been the official explanation.

'That is no excuse for closing down the whole establishment.' Mr Range pushed his steel spectacles back on his nose and hurried after Brazen. 'In the days when I was working closely with the Captain . . .'

'Days long gone, Mr Range.'

'He always said the climb back to knowledge would be painful . . .' They had arrived at one end of the workbench where a large device with illuminated dials was connected by wires to a huge carboy, rather like an oversized Chianti bottle. Mr Range stabbed a finger towards it. 'Devices like our electrical acid jar may seem trivial . . . to those old enough to remember the science we lost in the Day of Catastrophe. But we must follow the Long Path Captain Revere showed us. He taught us to make such things with our bare hands, and through that skill to change our destiny.'

The Orderly in front of the device seemed unconscious of their presence. The only sound that came through the headphones he wore was a constant numbing crackle, however much you manoeuvred the dials. Brazen abruptly unplugged the headphones. 'That'll do, Cockerill.'

Cockerill got up and stood slowly to attention as his commanding officer switched off the machine and ripped out the wires. Mr Range found fresh cause for complaint. 'You're abandoning the communications scan too!'

Brazen's reply was terse. 'Everything.'

Mr Range met Cockerill's eye, but found no ally there. The Orderly shrugged and said, 'Forty years, and nothing's come in on that set. I don't see it's any great loss.'

'No one invited your comment, Cockerill,' Brazen barked. 'You can resume corridor duty.' Cockerill saluted very smartly, turned on his heels and marched off.

Brazen was about to follow, but Mr Range began again on a

13

new note of urgency. 'Tell me one thing – on whose authority are you doing all this?'

'Plantagenet himself.'

Mr Range dismissed the idea with a shrug. 'The boy's distraught . . .'

'Are you suggesting the son of Captain Revere is not fit to rule?'

There was a warning note in Brazen's voice that made Mr Range tactfully change direction. 'As Chief Science Officer . . .'

'No good waving your title at me, Mr Range.' Brazen took his elbow and steered him firmly to the door. 'This research room is under military jurisdiction.' Mr Range had already noticed the armed Orderlies. The improvised long-barrelled shotguns they carried had been crafted from the ship's pressure distribution system. Ironically, Mr Range had designed them himself.

The scientist turned at the door to take stock of the big room, realising that he might be seeing it for the last time. A few of the smaller instruments and vessels remained, as well as the mineral samples arrayed along the shelves, back-lit by the dull greenish glow of the phosphor panels. Stripped of its furnishings it now looked less like the research room where in younger days he had worked as Captain Revere's assistant, and more like what it in fact was, the battered control room of a colony-ship, lying where it crashed forty years ago, half buried in the stony soil of Frontios.

Brazen edged Mr Range out into the corridor. Already a chain of colonists were passing the rocks that would be used to cement up the entrance. But for the persistent scientist the debate was still not over. 'The research into the bombardment . . . ? You must see the urgency of that. The attacks are coming almost daily now.'

The Chief Orderly had still not released his heavy grip on the scientist's arm. He bent down towards his ear. 'There'll be no further discussion of this in front of our people. The desertion rate is already unacceptable. With or without your permission, Mr Range, the research room will be sealed.'

For Tegan and Turlough, Frontios was still only a looming green shape on the viewing screen. If the Doctor had had his way they would never have arrived on it. 'We've seen enough,' he said firmly. 'Time's up.' He threw switches on the console, preparing to dematerialise.

Tegan was reluctant to tear herself away from the screen. 'What happens to them, Doctor?' The Doctor had let them come close enough to make out moving shapes, people crossing an open space between what looked like strange misshapen buildings.

'Knowledge has its limits,' said the Doctor, stretching a hand towards the Time Column switch. 'Even for Time Lords. Ours reaches this far and no further. We're at the edge of the Gallifreyan noosphere. . . .' But at exactly that moment a sudden dizzying motion caused the TARDIS to drop like a stone.

The Doctor grabbed at a lever on the console. 'The stabiliser's failing. We've got to get out of hover mode.'

The first lurch had left the three occupants shaken. Now the time-machine gave an enormous lunge, throwing them off balance. Turlough staggered to his feet, pointing excitedly at the viewer screen, where the panorama of Frontios was obscured by what looked like dense black rain. 'A meteorite storm?' he suggested.

The Doctor looked troubled. 'The TARDIS should be able to resist this sort of thing.' Another great shudder ran through the ship as the Doctor wrestled to return to time-travel mode.

All their efforts were in vain. Rattling its occupants like a dice in a box, the TARDIS continued dropping through space toward the forlorn planet of Frontios.

*

From his look-out point, a roughly constructed hut on the roof of a low stone building opposite the medical centre, the Warnsman had been alerted by the first signs: a darkening sky, and a distant, high-pitched whistling that seemed to emanate from every point on the horizon. Sometimes these omens came and went with nothing worse to follow, which indicated that Frontios would be spared that day, perhaps for several days to come. The Warnsman hoped today would be like that. But the attacks seemed to come more frequently now than he remembered them as a boy.

Below him, across the open space, a row of small improvised buildings – living accommodation, workshops, shelters – nestled under the curved hull of the wrecked colony-ship like a motley litter nuzzling some giant sow. The Warnsman stood rock-still, scanning the sky, his fist closed ready on the turning-handle of the klaxon. You gave the warning when you were certain, not before. For false warnings, the Captain had always taught, brought warnings into disregard.

The first black shapes appeared like drizzle on the horizon to the west. The moment he was certain, he applied both hands to the crank, turning it fast. The urgent croak of the klaxon lifted through several octaves and became a scream that split the air.

Without panic the Colonists of Frontios laid down their work and began to hurry towards the shelter of the buildings. Long experience had given them the measure of these emergencies. But today something was wrong. From his high perch the Warnsman noticed with alarm that the dark swirling bands of the approaching bombardment were sweeping forward with unnatural speed. He cranked the klaxon faster, his muscles cracking under the strain. But even before the first colonists had cleared the central space, the whistling of the onrush began to drown out the mechanical sound. The deadly hail was already falling.

In the scramble for cover there were casualties. A few of

the wounded lay in the open, vulnerable to the torrent that followed, and there was no helping them. By then the Warnsman himself had taken cover and the klaxon stood silent.

The medical shelter was the safest place to be on that unsafe planet, a low stone building that was mostly underground. Human forms jammed the entrance, and those that could get no further huddled against the stone walls outside.

In the darkness, noise and confusion none of the colonists noticed the largest of all the jetsam that descended from the sky. Raising a great whale-spout of dust as it jolted to a halt, there appeared in the middle of the open area a blue rectangular object, with darkly glazed windows in its upper part and a sign that said 'POLICE BOX', surmounted by a flashing blue light. The TARDIS had arrived on Frontios.

2

The Unknown Invaders

A blonde young woman dressed in the uniform of a paramedic pushed her way through the huddle of bodies to look
out through the doorway of the medical centre. The danger
was not entirely over: occasional missiles boomed down
onto the hull of the wrecked colony-ship, and any one of
them could kill. But the wounded had to be attended to,
and her father was already out in the open space working
under the protection of a metal hatch cover to take stock
and help the lucky survivors to safety.

Norna ran across the open space to him. Her path took
her within a few feet of the TARDIS, but her mind was
filled with busy thoughts of plasters and plasma and had no
room for such an absurdity. Perhaps this was as well, for the
sight of the Doctor's face peering out through the double
doors, as it did a moment after she had passed, would have
sent her hurrying back for shelter. Or perhaps have brought
her to a halt, helpless with laughter. Norna's reactions were
not always predictable.

The Doctor eyed the sky with evident distaste. 'My least
favourite sort of weather,' he muttered, and was about to
duck back inside again when he heard a moan. An injured
colonist was crawling on his hands and knees towards the
TARDIS.

When Mr Range and Norna returned to the medical

shelter with the walking wounded, the Doctor followed uninvited, carrying the injured colonist he had found. Behind him, Tegan and Turlough helped another of the wounded. The sky had cleared by now, and other colonists had mustered to help the injured.

The TARDIS crew arrived unnoticed at the medical shelter doorway. But the crush of people made it impossible for the Doctor to get in without asserting himself. In the normal way of things this was something he was reluctant to do, but now he did it loudly, out of regard for the injured man he was carrying.

Mr Range, oddly, accepted the presence of this complete stranger as perfectly natural in the circumstances, and helped clear the way. A flight of stone steps led steeply down from the doorway towards a kind of stone basement that was more like a primitive dungeon.

The Doctor was shocked at what he saw. 'What do you call this?'

'The medical shelter,' Mr Range replied. 'It's the best we can do.'

In beds and in pallets on the floor, wounded Frontios colonists seemed to occupy every available surface, while paramedics flitted between them. Tegan, following the Doctor and Mr Range down the steps, was struck once more by the Doctor's talent for getting on with people. The small man with steel spectacles, evidently a scientist of some kind, was already talking to him like a colleague.

'There's one really urgent case. Over here . . .' Mr Range led the Doctor over to one of the patients.

'Scalpels, retractors . . .' said the Doctor. 'I presume you've got all the tools.'

'Some. But we try to avoid invasive surgery. The recovery rate is very low.'

The Doctor glanced up at the high windows, which reached down thin fingers of light into the gloom. The

19

greenish glow of the hand-held phosphor lamps carried by the paramedics did little to cheer the scene. 'Yes, it would be . . . in here,' he said.

The Doctor's two companions had turned their own patient over to the paramedics. Tegan went to see if the Doctor needed any help, leaving Turlough to take a leisurely look round.

Paramedics bustled about with basins and bandages up and down the aisles between the beds, and wherever Turlough stood he seemed to be in somebody's way. He noticed a curious thing: despite the shortage of space, an arched niche on one grey stone wall was dominated by a large machine that did not seem to have been used for a long time.

The area behind the big home-made machine was just wide enough for a small office. The desk and filing cabinet suggested that someone was attempting to administer the chaos of the medical centre, or perhaps needed an excuse to escape from it from time to time.

Turlough stepped out of the niche on the other side to look at the engine – or whatever it was – from the front, and noticed a giant hand-painted portrait on the wall above. The face was etched with age but the eyes were strikingly bright, giving the man the look of a visionary. The portrait seemed to be all of a piece with the strange disused machine, like some exhibit in a museum.

'That's Captain Revere – or rather, was,' said a voice in his ear. He turned to see Mr Range pushing his spectacles back on his nose and offering his hand in greeting. 'The Doctor's about to do an operation, and needs your help.'

Turlough didn't know anything about operations, but was flattered to be asked. It turned out that the Doctor needed somebody to hold his coat. 'This lighting . . .' said the Doctor, rolling up his sleeves, 'is more like darking. Unless I can see more of the patient, I'm likely to make an incision in the mattress.'

Mr Range took a lamp from one of the paramedics and brought it closer. 'Without the resources to create filaments and vacuums these are the best we can manage.'

Turlough grabbed another of the lamps and looked at it closely. 'These things are banned on Circle Link Group planets.' He shook it, and the green glow brightened suddenly. 'Emergency phosphor lamps! Terrible fire hazard in these sort of containers!'

'Then hold it steady,' snapped the Doctor.

'Batteries, or what?' Tegan asked.

'Direct electron excitation. It gets brighter every time you . . .' Turlough shook the lamp vigorously this time, and it began to shine white hot.

'Stop that!' shouted the Doctor, who knew the hazards of phosphor lamps better than anybody. He took the dangerous device from the young man and gave it to one of the paramedics, and it became quickly subdued to its normal unhelpful glow. The Doctor wished he could have a hundred Turloughs shaking phosphor lamps to chase the shadows out of that grim hospital. . . . Or perhaps a single 100 Turlough lamp . . . His mind began to muse upon the possibilities of portable equipment in the TARDIS. Yes, that was it. He prodded Turlough and pointed to the door. 'TARDIS – the mu-field activator . . . and about five of the argon discharge globes.'

'But . . .' said Turlough, typically.

'Go!' said the Doctor, returning his own monosyllable with a conviction that brooked no argument. Turlough shrugged and pushed his way down the aisle.

'. . . And a laser scalpel . . .' the Doctor called after him, but the young man was already striding up the stairs. The Doctor turned to Tegan. 'You know where all the medical stuff is . . .'

'OK, Doctor,' she said with a smile, and hurried off after Turlough.

★

Emerging from the medical shelter, Tegan was grateful for the fresh air. Turlough slowed his pace to let her catch up. Ahead of them a small group of Orderlies and colonists had gathered in curiosity around the TARDIS. But as the two companions approached the group withdrew to a distance, whispering among themselves.

'I thought we weren't supposed to be interfering on this planet,' said Turlough in his superior public school tone. 'Time Laws, and all that.'

'You know the Doctor,' Tegan replied. 'Once he gets interested, the rules go on the junk heap.'

They pulled open the double doors of the TARDIS and went inside. Neither of them realised at that stage that the planet might be interfering with them. But they were on the point of discovering the first dangerous signs.

The huge high arch of metal, crumpled by the terrible collision, lent a kind of gothic majesty to the jet vent's new role as the sole entrance to the wrecked colony-ship. Brazen had come out onto the ramp at the urgent summons of his Deputy, who was now pointing across the open area towards the TARDIS.

Brazen's face darkened. From the Deputy's description it had sounded like another of the wild speculations that were dangerous to the security of Frontios, not because they were true but because they were believed. But there was no doubting the reality of this mysterious blue object. Brazen turned on his heel and re-entered the colony-ship, flicking his fingers to the Deputy to accompany him. The improvised double doors that now protected the entrance were slammed and bolted shut behind them, and the guards on duty hitched up their long shot-guns and resumed their watch.

The footsteps of Brazen and his Deputy sent melancholy echoes booming through the propulsion chamber. Whether this new phenomenon in the open area outside was of alien origin as the rumours claimed was something only close inspection would reveal. Brazen's immediate duty was to muster the current facts, get a grip on the situation, make a report.

The propulsion chamber led them through into Causeway 8 that ran the length of the ship – a half hour's brisk walk in the days Brazen was a boy and the ship was whole. Now most of the structure except the stern end was buckled and filled with silt, and only the part of the ship they walked in now was usable for the business of state and the storage of the precious resource reserves.

They turned off into a narrower walkway. Cockerill, the Orderly relieved of communications duty, was standing guard outside one of the doors. He shook his head as the Chief Orderly approached. 'He's in the State Room.'

'He? What do you mean – he!' Brazen's voice snapped back like a whip. 'Plantagenet, if you please, Cockerill. We'll use his name with respect. A leader is a leader.'

Cockerill drew himself to attention, and Brazen and his Deputy walked on to the State Room in the next section. Brazen knocked respectfully and, signalling to the Deputy to wait outside, went in.

The room was lit by a pair of large luminous panels emitting the same pale greenish glow as the phosphor lamps. No light came from a matching third panel where the translucent material covering was cracked, a reminder, like the broken instrumentation around the walls, of the catastrophe the ship had suffered. This room had been the control centre, the reins that gave mere humans command over the ship's entire technological resources, power that now was only a memory for the handful of survivors.

Sitting in the state chair, part of his father's paraphernalia of government, Plantagenet did not look like a leader. His youth and thin physique were partly to blame for this impression. But there was also his obvious physical fear for his own safety, although the sound of the bombardment had long since died away.

Brazen closed the door. 'There's a development, sir, which I'm not happy with.'

Plantagenet cleared his throat. 'Development? Yes?'

'Apparently an arrival.' No point in presenting the news in a complicated fashion, Brazen had decided. It would be regarded as an alien object until proved otherwise. 'Simultaneous to the last bombardment. Three persons of undetermined origin.'

Plantagenet straightened himself. His hands were shaking; he clasped them behind his back and tried to control the quaver in his voice. 'You mean . . . it's come at last?'

'As you say, sir. A possibility.'

The young leader closed his eyes for a moment, trying to contact something within himself that offered the promise of strength. It was the sense of inevitability, of history directing him precisely to this point of time and nowhere else, that held out some faint hope of freeing the tightness around his heart. In the great unfolding of time, one small human terror is a mote of dust.

He opened his eyes and walked towards the door, signalling Brazen to follow.

As Mr Range had suggested, the Doctor was trying to keep the treatment as non-invasive as possible, but some of the injuries were so bad that a certain amount of cutting and rebuilding of tissue was inevitable.

'It's very good of you to help, Mr . . .' said Mr Range, fishing for the umpteenth time for the Doctor's name.

'I'm not helping . . . officially. And if anybody happens to ask you whether I made any material difference to the welfare of this planet . . . Retractor! . . . you can tell them I came and went like a summer cloud.'

As he looked up to take the retractor from Norna he noticed the gathering of colonists at the top of the steps, who were watching the progress of the operation with an

24

interest that did not seem entirely friendly. He waved to the paramedics to send them away. 'They're blocking the air.'

Mr Range dropped his voice. 'Don't antagonise them, it could be dangerous. They're wondering where you come from.'

'It's where these come from that intrigues me.' The Doctor locked off the retractor and gently withdrew the forceps from the wound. The foreign body gripped in its jaws was something like a small distorted stone.

Mr Range shook his head. 'No one has managed to determine the origin of the bombardment.'

The Doctor held the fragment under the light of the phosphor lamp. 'Hmmm . . . some sort of very dense . . .' Suddenly Mr Range's curious choice of words struck him a delayed blow. 'Bombardment?'

'You saw it for yourself, Doctor. The attacks have become frequent these past few weeks.'

'You're at war? This is a regular thing?'

Mr Range nodded. 'And without our technology we're helpless . . .'

The Doctor passed the forceps over to Norna and reached for his coat, extending his other hand to Mr Range to shake. 'Not if I have anything to do with it, Mr Range.' He nodded to the paramedic at his side, leaving him to close the wound.

Delighted that the long-awaited introduction might now be taking place, Mr Range gripped the Doctor's hand warmly. 'Your name, sir.'

'The Doctor,' said the Doctor.

'Doctor . . . ?' quizzed Mr Range.

'The,' said the Doctor. 'They just call me the Doctor.' But his attention, never gripped by formalities such as these, had already drifted to something over Mr Range's shoulder in the gloom behind. 'You've been keeping us unnecessarily in the dark, Mr Range,' the Doctor exclaimed, moving over towards the strange neglected

25

engine that Turlough had already discovered. 'You didn't tell me you had a hydrazine steam generator.'

'Oh yes. It generated a very basic form of energy, before the fuel ran out,' said Mr Range, and began rather unnecessarily pointing out the salient features of the machine.

The Doctor nodded. 'Electricity, yes. That must have been good for something.'

'Unfortunately not. We had nothing it could drive.' The news took the Doctor by surprise. 'But your colony-ship. It must have been positively brimming with gadgetry.'

Mr Range smiled ruefully, remembering the past splendour. 'Systems that would rebuild a civilisation for us. Failure-proof technology.'

'Well,' prompted the Doctor when Mr Range fell silent. 'What happened to it all?'

Mr Range sighed. 'It failed! Nothing survived the crash!'

Any further thoughts Mr Range might have had on the subject were interrupted by the arrival of Tegan and Turlough, who came tumbling down the steps, calling to the Doctor. 'The TARDIS,' said Tegan. 'Doctor, something's happened to it.'

The Doctor was still dwelling on what Mr Range had told him, and merely looked vague when Tegan and Turlough arrived at his side, both talking at once. 'It's as if some tremendous force-field's pulled it out of shape,' said Turlough.

'The interior door's jammed,' Tegan interrupted. 'It couldn't be the impact of landing, could it?'

Important though the TARDIS was to him, the Doctor's mind remained entangled in his own elaborate thoughts. 'The TARDIS?' he replied with a shrug. 'Probably just some . . . spatial anomaly. . . .' The exotic geometry of his time-machine seemed to him at that moment of rarefied theoretical interest beside the pressing problems of Frontios. Not least the problem of the lighting. He picked up a phosphor lamp and shook it gently, an idea forming in his mind. 'You're getting carried away again, Turlough. One thing at a time. Where's the mu-field activator?'

Turlough did not bother to conceal his irritation. 'I'm trying to tell you. It's on the other side . . .'

'. . . of the interior door . . .' interrupted the Doctor, to show Turlough that he had been listening to every word. 'Yes, I see the difficulty.' Absent-mindedly he shook the phosphor lamp vigorously until it burned with a fierce white light. 'Excitation! Have you ever put a high voltage across one of these things?'

'You told him not to do that . . .' Tegan pointed out.

But the Doctor wasn't listening. 'It's risky. But so is operating in this gloom.' He turned to Mr Range. 'There must be something on this planet that can sustain a permanent voltage . . .'

His voice tailed away as his gaze fell on the hydrazine steam generator. He threw a glance in the direction of Mr Range, inviting him to follow as he walked around behind the huge apparatus. Turlough was about to go with them, but the Doctor did not seem to invite his presence. So he stayed and asked Norna, 'How can you work . . . do research without electricity?'

'Captain Revere was using an acid jar. Charged by wind-power. We used it to drive the communications scanner.'

'What's an acid jar?' asked Tegan.

'A kind of large battery,' said Turlough, and suddenly became very excited, a different person from the young man who had spent long afternoons tying fierce knots in the Doctor's old scarves. He seemed confident that if they could find something to use as an interrupter, they could raise the voltage to deliver just what the Doctor needed.

'It's heavy, and tricky to carry,' said Norna. At this hint of physical rather than purely intellectual work Turlough seemed about to back-pedal. But with a brisk 'Come on',

Tegan grabbed him by the arm and the three of them hurried off up the steps.

The crowd of curious colonists that had gathered around the TARDIS now formed a ragged queue on the other side of the open space. Outside the entrance to the crashed colony-ship, food was being dispensed from trestle tables, a diet of rough dark bread shaped into cubes, and what smelled to Turlough's discerning nose like root vegetable stew. 'Food is rationed on Frontios,' Norna explained, and pointed to the huge double doors that led into the colony-ship. Turlough had already noticed the unfriendly guards manning the entrance. 'They store everything edible or useful in there.'

'That explains the shotguns,' Tegan said.

Turlough hesitated, an unpleasant thought forming in his mind. 'You don't intend to get us in there, I hope?'

'If you want the acid jar . . .' said Norna. 'Scientific resources are banned since the research room was closed, so we might have to be devious about this.'

Turlough laughed hollowly, and glanced again at the shotguns the guards were carrying. It occurred to him that being cooped up in the TARDIS for weeks on end wasn't such a bad existence after all. Then as he watched, the guards suddenly jumped to attention, and the double doors opened for Plantagenet and Brazen, who emerged from the colony-ship attended by two Orderlies.

Norna dragged them out of the queue to the cover of a pile of abandoned crates lined up along the hull of the great ship. 'Quiet! Stay here a moment and leave this to me.'

Plantagenet glanced uneasily at the sky in a momentary lapse from courage. Brazen touched his arm. 'Stand steady, sir. They look to you.' The food queue had indeed turned in their direction, the stew temporarily neglected for this rare sight of the new young leader. A young girl, her blonde hair streaming behind her, was striding toward the colony-ship entrance.

'Norna,' said Plantagenet. 'You're needed in the hospital, surely?'

'I've come to ask for bandages and water,' said Norna, stopping at the bottom of the ramp that led to the jet vent.

The reply came from Brazen; resource management was his concern. 'You think we have unlimited supplies?'

Norna was unabashed by this official intervention. 'You have supplies. What's the good of hoarding them?' Out of the corner of her eye she could see Tegan and Turlough crouching behind the crates, waiting for her signal. 'Leader Plantagenet – the wounded colonists need our help.'

This shrewd appeal of Norna's touched Plantagenet on the raw. He whispered to Brazen, who then beckoned to one of the armed guards to step forward. 'Take her to the medical supplies room,' Brazen said. And with a nod to Norna, he and Plantagenet moved off towards the TARDIS with a pair of escorting Orderlies.

Norna ran her fingers through her hair – the signal to her two new friends. Tegan picked one of the smaller empty crates and balanced it on her shoulder. She made her way round towards the entrance, being careful to keep her face hidden from the guards. Turlough tried to pick up a rather larger crate, but it was full of something heavy, and quite immovable. Tegan stole a glance back and saw him pulling at the crates one by one, still looking for one he could carry. She hesitated. The guards were getting ready to close the door behind them. Then suddenly from the direction of the crates came a crashing sound, the clatter of engine spares tumbling to the ground.

Two of the armed Orderlies on the door moved swiftly to investigate, running down the ramp and along the outside of the line of crates. From her vantage point Tegan could just see through the narrow gap between the high pile of crates and the hull of the ship. Turlough, aware of the danger he was in, was deftly making his way towards her.

The third armed Orderly, more slow-moving than the

29

others, had gone on ahead into the colony-ship. Now he turned, and would have been sure to see Turlough in the next second. But Norna was swift-thinking. 'Give him the crate,' she snapped at Tegan. Tegan thrust the crate on the surprised Orderly, obligingly freeing his hands by taking his shotgun. At the same moment Turlough was squeezing through the narrow gap, and had climbed onto the ramp and joined his two friends before the Orderly knew what was happening. By the time the Orderly had put down the crate and recovered his rifle, the entrance was empty.

The commotion had also attracted Brazen's interest. He left Plantagenet and came back to look at the spilled spare parts. 'Who occasioned this spillage?' he asked the two Orderlies poking among the crates. They didn't know; they suspected an intruder. Brazen turned his head dully towards the colony-ship entrance where the armed guard stood preparing to close the heavy metal doors. Any unauthorised personnel who got in would have great difficulty in getting out again.

Following Norna, Tegan and Turlough walked swiftly through the propulsion chamber until they came to a great wide corridor that was Causeway 8. 'There are a lot of patrols here,' Norna said. 'We'd better go the long way round to the research room. Follow me.'

They ran with her across the Causeway into a narrow alleyway where the lighting was dim and they were able to pause to catch their breath. 'This place,' said Tegan. 'It's huge!'

'It brought thousands of people from Earth, remember,' Norna said.

Of course, a colony-ship would have to carry a huge number of people. But if there were once thousands of them . . .

'Most of the population died immediately in the crash,' said Norna unemotionally. It was not that she felt no sadness for her grandparents and the rest of the brave pioneers from Earth. But it was a long time ago, before she was born. 'And with no life support systems there was disease . . .'

Suddenly there was a shout from the direction of the Causeway, and the sound of fast-moving feet coming towards them. 'Run for it!' exclaimed Norna under her breath, and set off down the alleyway.

Mr Range looked nervously around at the occupants of the medical shelter. The paramedics had paused in their work, and the patients who were able were sitting up – all watching the Doctor with growing mistrust. He had climbed up onto the generator, and was peering down into a section he had dismantled, drawing a sketch on a notepad that he had already covered with writing and figures.

'A neat job, this,' the Doctor called down to Mr Range. 'Cannibalised from the colony-ship's hydraulic system.'

'Captain Revere built it,' explained Mr Range, when the Doctor had reached ground level again and was busily retrieving his coat. 'We preserve it as a monument to the Long Path ahead.' He explained about the Long Path of knowledge that Captain Revere had taught them needed to be travelled before their civilisation could thrive again.

The Doctor was more concerned with the immediate present than with ideologies and the future, but he waited patiently for Mr Range to finish before handing over the sketch he had made. 'I've modified the interrupter. A spot of elementary Time Mechanics. Not a word, mind. . . . All we need now is a reliable low-voltage source.' He patted the machine. 'If this is the sum total of your technology, Mr Range . . . this war you're involved in must be a trifle one-sided.'

'And quite senseless.'

'All wars are,' said the Doctor feelingly. 'But I never knew one without a purpose.'

Mr Range responded willingly to the implied question.

'Captain Revere assumed the barrage must be some sort of softening-up process. Heralding an invasion, he said.'

But as it appeared that the planet was deserted when the colonists arrived, this didn't fit any pattern of aggression the Doctor had encountered before. 'You did nothing to provoke an attack from surrounding planets. No high tech developments, of course?'

'After the Day of Catastrophe we few who lived had no time for anything but bare survival. We worked to raise food.' That was before the bombardments began. Mr Range told the Doctor of the ten years of clear skies that gave them a chance to stock the wreck of the colony-ship with food – Captain Revere's plan to give the colonists time for their real task.

'The Long Path thing, yes . . .' said the Doctor. 'But look, Mr Range, if I'm understanding this time scheme right . . . the first of the missiles must have fallen a little more than thirty years ago. Your unknown invaders are certainly taking their time.'

It was not Mr Range who replied. The Doctor was startled by an interruption from the top of the steps. The newcomer stood in the doorway, his face in shadow, but the light streaming in behind him accentuated his head of thick, white hair. The Doctor could make out the outline of a thin young man, no older than Turlough, wearing regalia that marked him out as a leader. Hedged about him were Orderlies carrying dangerous long-barrelled primitive shotguns.

'Unknown no longer, perhaps,' said Plantagenet. 'Could it be that one of them calls himself the Doctor?'

3

The Deadly Hail

There were intruders in the colony-ship, and the alarm had
been raised. But at that moment the only occupant of the
State Room was more concerned with the half chicken he
had managed to filch from the officers' galley. Cockerill
slouched in Plantagenet's big chair, one leg slung over the
arm, savouring the all too infrequent delicacy.

The sound of running feet in the corridor did not disturb
him until it stopped outside the door. A man of quick
reflexes when the occasion demanded, Cockerill was on his
feet before the door opened, the chicken vanished from
sight, and he was an alert Orderly attending the return of
the leader. But it was not the leader.

Norna, Tegan and Turlough slipped into the room and
shut the door. The three friends leant against it, catching
their breath as the sound of other feet raced by outside. At
first they did not see Cockerill.

'The State Room,' said Norna to the others. 'We won't be
very safe here.'

'Correct!' said a new voice that made them jump.
Cockerill had approached within a few feet of them. A tall
man, quietly spoken, but nonetheless a menacing figure for
them at that moment.

But before they could say anything, the Orderly went on
in a much more friendly tone, 'But then what is safe on this

33

hope-forsaken planet?' Incongruously a chicken wing appeared in his hand and he began to munch. 'Security must be at an all time low, if a bunch of kids can just wander into the State Room.'

Moments later Cockerill put his head out of the State Room door and checked that the corridor was empty. At a signal from him the three friends followed him out of the room. 'Off you go,' he said cheerfully. 'And I never saw you.'

Norna hesitated. 'Why are you doing this?'

Cockerill shrugged. 'If I understood long words like "why" . . . I wouldn't just be an Orderly.' With that he disappeared back into the State Room, leaving Norna, Tegan and Turlough with the feeling they had met someone remarkable. But none of them guessed how very extraordinary Cockerill would turn out to be.

They kept up a brisk pace, going the long way round through corridors that seemed to get narrower and narrower. They came to a companionway, steep steps that disappeared into a dark funnel in the ceiling. Their eyes had become accustomed to the dim green light of the corridors, but now they left it behind as they climbed, and for a while the darkness was almost total. Then came the creaking of neglected metal fittings and a blinding whiteness as Norna opened the bulkhead. It was the sky.

They found themselves standing on a horizontal surface punctuated by vertical structures: loading machinery, ballast tanks and strangely finned exhaust ports. Long abandoned by repair teams, the silver hull was pitted everywhere from the impact of countless bombardments, the metal cladding even ripped open in places.

Norna was about to close the bulkhead when she heard, echoing up the companionway, the sound of a patrol – three or four of them moving swiftly in the corridor below. In her haste the door slipped from her fingers at the last moment, slamming home with a metallic shudder.

She got to her feet. 'We'd better hurry. But be careful.' Tegan and Turlough followed her quickly along a twisted walkway, and after a moment they came to an almost concealed hatch let into the hull. Norna began tugging on it urgently, and eventually Turlough had to come to her help, after fastidiously wrapping a handkerchief around his hand against the rust.

Tegan had hung back to look out for pursuers, peeping through the rust-riddled shell of a fuel tank. Now she came running up to them, whispering and gesturing. 'They're coming.' With her help the hatch at last creaked open, giving them barely time to slip inside and close it behind them, before heavy footfalls announced the arrival of the Orderlies.

They found themselves clinging like flies to a stunted ladder that descended a little way into the centre of a large deserted room. It stopped short of a horizontal beam that ran the length of the ceiling. Norna wriggled down towards it, stretching across to reach the block and tackle that hung from it.

From his perch on the ladder Turlough could hear feet shifting on the metal structure overhead. Brazen's voice called, 'Check the solar drive panels. They've got to be hiding out here somewhere.' Then after a moment came the welcome sound of footsteps receding along the hull.

The girls had already reached the floor, and were manhandling some large object towards the hook of the block and tackle. 'It smells lethal,' whispered Tegan.

'It is,' Norna said. 'So please don't spill it.' Inside the green glass carboy Tegan noticed an elaborate maze of metallic plates submersed in a thick liquid. Acrid fumes rose from the open neck as the bottle was stirred by the motion of manoeuvring it towards the hook. They took their time hitching it to the block and tackle, ignoring the hurry-up gestures from Turlough up on his high perch.

Norna stepped back to let Tegan take the weight on the rope. But the block and tackle did not run smoothly; Tegan's steady pull became a jerk that sent the thick smoking liquid into a shiver. She jumped back as a little of the acid spilled from the neck – a move that would have sent the whole jar crashing to the floor if Norna hadn't grabbed the rope and held it steady.

On the floor by their feet the little pool of acid sizzled like hot fat, burning an indentation into the metal plate.

Brazen returned to the bulkhead, puzzled at the disappearance of his quarry. A secure area for essential supplies and administration was crucial to the maintenance of order, and the ship was barely adequate for the purpose – too large to guard with a small force of men.

The hull commanded a good view of the sand dunes around the settlement. Brazen thought of the Retrograde deserters living out in that barren country like animals in burrows. As their numbers grew, raiding parties like these would become more common.

'Kernighan . . . Ritchie . . . See nobody passes through here,' he instructed the Orderlies. 'I'll appraise the leader of this development.' Brazen clambered down the companionway.

He was hurrying past the blocked up entrance to the Research Room, when he heard a tuneless whistling approaching down the corridor. It was Cockerill, walking towards him with his hands in his pockets.

'Are you on duty, Cockerill?' Cockerill straightened up. 'Then deport yourself like an Orderly. You look more like one of those hope-forsaken Retrogrades.' The Orderly snapped to attention with an exaggeration that Brazen vaguely sensed was intended as an insult. 'Yes, sir. I was on my way to assist Kernighan and Ritchie. There's an alert.'

'I initiated it, Cockerill. Get out on the hull, man – and do that jacket up!'

Cockerill put his fingers to the buttons, but the Chief Orderly, preoccupied with matters of general security, had already marched off down the corridor. Cockerill breathed a sigh of relief. With its additional burden of contraband his jacket would not have fastened.

Kernighan opened the bulkhead in response to the knocking. 'Got it,' said Cockerill, climbing out onto the hull. 'But only just.' He emptied out the feast of cooked chicken and bread, negotiated from stores with considerable diplomacy and the kind of gentle blackmail Orderlies could always exert over non-commissioned colonists.

Fifty yards away Turlough was watching the share-out from the cover of a bulwark. 'How are we going to get it past them?' asked Tegan. Cockerill and his two companions had settled down to their meal in a way that suggested they would be there for some time. After the difficulty they had had manoeuvring the acid jar out onto the hull, the picnic was a far from welcome sight.

It was Norna who came up with the idea. Working as quietly as they could they dragged the block and tackle out onto the hull, its end still attached to its original mooring in the research room. Turlough looked over the edge of the hull. The ground seemed a long way away, and the little low stone buildings that circled the open area were like dolls' houses. 'Are you sure this is safe?' he asked.

Tegan and Norna were dragging the acid jar to the edge of the hull. 'As safe as it's ever likely to be,' said Tegan abruptly. 'Come on, lend us a hand.'

Over their heads the sky was starting to darken. If Norna had noticed she might have changed her mind about risking the long descent in the open, but she was too busy securing the neck of the acid jar to the hook of the block and tackle.

One man, standing at his post on the roof of a low stone building in the settlement below them, did notice however. It was the Warnsman's job to notice. As Brazen crossed the open space on his way towards the medical shelter, the Warnsman called down to him, 'I don't like the look of this sky, Chief Orderly.'

Brazen looked up, his mind on other matters. To his soldier's eye the sky did not seem particularly perilous. 'Keep good watch,' he called back with a casual wave.

The Warnsman watched Brazen disappear into the low stone building. Then, shading his eyes. he lifted his face towards the sky again. But something on the way attracted his attention – tiny figures clambering over the edge of the great disabled colony-ship. A memory came back to him from decades ago, when as a child he watched men go out on ropes like that to inspect the hull. There had been wild talk then of using the undamaged plates to create a new ship. . . .

There are times for quiet explanation, but now was not one of them. Or so the Doctor decided, looking across at the ugly shotguns the Orderlies had unhitched from their shoulders and now held at the ready. At first there had been the usual conceptual difficulties in explaining to Plantagenet how they came to be on his planet – and how they had managed to survive the bombardment when they were caught up in it. The final straw had been the discovery of the Doctor's experiments with the hydrazine steam engine – a rather ordinary machine, the Doctor thought, which they seemed to regard as a sort of sacred relic of Captain Revere.

Mr Range was now busily polishing his glasses in a flurry of embarrassment. But then the little scientist did a remarkable thing. He put the glasses on again, took a deliberate step towards Plantagenet and shouted very loudly directly at the young leader, 'This is nonsense. Sheer paranoia. Our minds are being eaten away by this daily disaster we call Frontios. To the few of us remaining sane it's as clear as daylight – this man is here to help us.'

Despite the tension in the air, the weapons of Plantagenet's cohorts remained shouldered, and the young leader's tone was still controlled and icily polite. He pointed a finger at Mr Range. 'I say treachery, Mr Range. Are you guilty too?'

The Doctor intervened in as calm a voice as he could muster. 'Look here, everybody. We can clear this up in no time, if we all keep calm. Come and see the TARDIS.'

'TARDIS?' The word came from Plantagenet, but everyone within earshot turned to the Doctor with the same question.

'My ship . . . Well, not exactly mine, but that's a long story. You're all welcome to look it over. As an invasion weapon you'll have to agree it's about as offensive as a chicken vol-au-vent. . . .'

With a nonchalance that quite disconcerted the cohorts of Orderlies, the Doctor headed for the steps, waving at Plantagenet to follow him. Unfortunately the door was thrown open before he reached it, and Brazen blocked the way.

'Wait,' said the Chief Orderly, summoning a pair of shotgun carriers to guard the door. He stamped down the steps for a whispered conference with Plantagenet, and a moment later the Doctor found himself being forcibly led back to Plantagenet.

'You arrived with two accomplices,' came the accusation. 'They have been seen in the colony-ship.' Plantagenet's reserve had finally cracked, and the anger welled out. He turned to Mr Range. 'Aided by your treacherous daughter.'

The rope dragged at the skin of Turlough's palms as he steadied it against the weight. Over the edge of the hull he could just make out the shapes of the two girls clinging to it, their feet in knotted loopholes. Below them the acid jar hung from its hook a perilous distance above the ground. From the other side of the bulwark he could hear the conversation of Cockerill and the other two Orderlies enjoying their picnic. They were far too close for comfort, and Turlough's only thought was to finish the job quickly and shin down to ground level.

It was the custom for the Warnsman when the sky was clear to leave his post to make a round of the settlement. Now as he stood under the great cathedral shape of the colony-ship, he began to doubt the wisdom of his decision. He had been misled by Brazen's casual estimate of the sky: the gloom was rapidly thickening, and at any moment he expected to hear the first whistling sounds of a new bombardment.

The little matchstick figures and the rope he had seen from his lookout post must have been a trick of the light, he decided, and he was heading back to be ready with the klaxon when, rounding a bend of the hull, he heard a shout from above.

'Get back. It's dangerous!' But Norna's warning came too late. The acid jar, swinging perilously above his head, lurched downward and caught him a sharp crack behind the ear. He stumbled and fell to the ground; drops of acid, narrowly missing his head, sizzled into the soil. Norna jumped from the rope and knelt over him.

Up on the hull Turlough had been surprised to hear the conversation of the picnickers stop suddenly, interrupted by a voice that he knew to be Cockerill's saying, 'That's it. . . . Listen, it's coming.'

Turlough listened too, and fancied he heard a faint whistling noise coming from all points of the compass. Then to his surprise he heard the Orderlies abandoning their picnic and scrambling in through the bulkhead door, slamming it after them. A split second later he knew the reason for their panic, when the first of the missiles fell onto the hull with an ominous hollow thud.

Eventually the Doctor managed to persuade Brazen and Plantagenet at least to look at the TARDIS before taking

40

any drastically irreversible action, like discharging one of the wicked-looking guns in his direction. 'I give you my personal guarantee the TARDIS is not an instrument of war,' he assured them as they made their way out of the medical shelter. 'Its lack of armaments are a positive embarrassment at times . . .' He broke off to pick up something from the ground. 'Just a minute . . .' It lay in the palm of his hand, an innocent-seeming translucent stone. 'Still warm . . . GET BACK!'

The Doctor pushed Plantagenet back under the cover. Brazen stood in the doorway, scanning the sky. 'We've heard nothing from the Warnsman.'

'No wonder . . .' said the Doctor. 'Is that him?'

They turned to see Turlough helping the injured Warnsman across the open space towards them. Behind him, Tegan and Norna struggled with the acid jar.

Ignoring the guns pointed in his direction, the Doctor ran to them. 'What do you think you're doing?' Norna explained quickly about the battery. 'Brilliant,' said the Doctor. 'Or at least it will be. But our immediate problem is the bombardment. . . . Come on, hurry.' Waving imperiously to the Orderlies to take care of the acid jar he picked up the Warnsman and carried him to the door of the shelter.

Norna was helping the Orderlies down the steps with the acid jar when the klaxon sounded outside. Suddenly there was a flurry of people pushing in at the door, and Mr Range had to run up the steps to help keep the jar steady. The Doctor handed the injured man over to him, then reached through the jostling crowd to catch Tegan's hand. 'Where's Turlough?' he shouted. She pointed outside, and the two of them ran to the door.

The open space had now become a blur of rushing figures, all sound drowned by the noise of the missiles and the klaxon's harsh shriek. They found Turlough pressed against the wall looking across towards the TARDIS. 'I was thinking that too,' said the Doctor, seeing the expression on

Turlough's face. 'A swift exit. We've had enough of this planet.'

But as they struggled through the rush of colonists it quickly became obvious they had no chance of reaching safety in that direction. The Doctor grabbed his two companions and wheeled them around. 'Quick, under cover.'

The door to the medical shelter was jammed with people. But under the sloping hull of the colony ship there were places where the soil had been eroded to form shallow hollows, and many of the colonists were already crouching there like rats in the skirting-board.

During what seemed like hours crouched with the Doctor and Turlough under the hull of the colony-ship, Tegan thought of home. The routine of airline duties didn't seem so bad if this chaos of noise and hideous injury was the alternative. The missiles hailing down on the plate-work over their heads blended into a continuous metallic thunder that made her head reel.

And then, like a diminishing drum roll, the sound slowed to a halt. Between the Doctor's shoulder and the arch of the ship's hull, Tegan could see a patch of rapidly clearing sky. The Doctor shifted on his elbow, straightening a leg that had gone to sleep. 'That seems to be that for the moment,' he concluded. 'Everybody all right?'

They crawled out from the makeshift shelter. 'We'd better evacuate before the shotguns come out again,' said the Doctor. 'Come on, the TARDIS.'

It seemed a sensible suggestion to Tegan, though she could hardly think for the ringing in her ears. They set off at a brisk trot, following the Doctor in what seemed like the wrong direction. Looking round for the TARDIS, Tegan noticed Plantagenet, Brazen and their retinue of armed Orderlies emerging from the medical shelter.

The Doctor stopped abruptly. He was standing by a heap of rubble, staring dully at what looked at first like a stubbly tree with curling, leafless branches. It was the hat-stand, its foot invisible under the clutter of stones. A very unpleasant feeling came over Tegan. 'The TARDIS . . . What's happened?'

'It's gone,' said the Doctor, in a voice that sounded like the far end of a bad telephone line. 'The TARDIS has been destroyed!'

Dimly at the edge of their suddenly shrunken world the steel nuzzles of shotguns pressed in like a circle of curious pigs.

4

The Power of the Hat-stand

Tegan stared aghast at the half-buried hat-stand. 'But the TARDIS can't just vanish.'

'Well, it has!' Turlough snapped back, his nerves not helped by the armed guards closing in around them.

'Don't be stupid,' Tegan persisted, as if some fine point of logic were being overlooked. 'I know the TARDIS. It's just . . . gone into non-visual mode . . . or something.'

'You mean "vanished",' retorted the young man triumphantly. In attempting to keep her head through this terrible discovery Tegan was thoroughly confused by now. 'Yes . . . No . . .'

The Doctor had been mooching around the hat-stand, clenching and unclenching his fists to control his anger at this completely intolerable turn of events. 'No bickering, you two. We must take this like Time Lords.'

'It's her fault,' said Turlough.

'And we'll have no laying of blame.' With a nod towards the hostile-looking gathering, the Doctor added, 'It gives a bad impression.' He cleared his throat and turned to the crowd. 'Excuse my companions. They're upset. Well, naturally. I'm upset myself. Very, very upset. The Time Lords will be upset too – I was always meaning to return that TARDIS. Well, eventually . . .' He broke off from this not entirely coherent monologue, noticing a movement from one of the Orderlies. The man's left arm was a stump to the elbow, and now at a nod from Brazen, he was lifting it to steady his shotgun against his right shoulder.

'Marvellous!' said the Doctor, throwing up his hands in noisy exasperation. 'You're going to kill me. What a finely-tuned response to the situation.' He rounded on Turlough and Tegan. 'You see what you've got us into. If you hadn't insisted on hovering this would never had happened. . . .'

'Time Lords, Doctor,' said Turlough, reminding him of his own good advice. The Doctor let out a snort, and casting about for something to release his frustration on, gave the unfortunate hat-stand a mighty kick. A flurry of small sparks scattered over the ground, as if he had disturbed a nest of fireflies.

Plantagenet paled at the sight and looked uncertainly towards Brazen. The Chief Orderly caught him by the shoulder, and nodding towards the stump-armed man whose shotgun still covered the Doctor, though now from a little further back, he advised in a low voice, 'Best to despatch him now.'

'Wait!' Norna had been pushing her way through the crowd and now ran out in front of the young ruler. Despite Plantagenet's command to step out of the way, she refused to be intimidated. 'Just tell me this,' she said in a voice that the whole crowd could hear. 'Why did Captain Revere dedicate his life to analysing the rocks of Frontios? Up to the day he died?'

Plantagenet was statesman enough to see that this challenge had to be met. 'Why do you ask, Norna, when the reason is well known to all of Frontios? My father sought the precious minerals beneath the soil.'

The young girl did not flinch. 'What precious minerals? Did he find any?'

'He knew there must be some cause for this perpetual carnage our neighbours inflict on us.' The guards about him nodded. It was common knowledge that the invaders must

45

know of treasures under the soil. What other reason could there be for this protracted war?

'If the Doctor is an invader,' Norna replied simply, 'he has the answer to that question.'

In the silence all eyes turned to the Doctor. But Mr Range had been elbowing his way to the front of the crowd, and now he intervened, anxious to disentangle his daughter from the incident. 'Norna, I need some help with the lighting . . .'

Brazen stopped him with a gesture, and bent his head to whisper to Plantagenet. The young ruler listened, then suddenly pointed at Tegan. 'You go.'

'I don't know anything about lighting,' Tegan said loudly. 'If I'm going anywhere, it's home.'

'I'm afraid with no TARDIS . . . this is home,' said the Doctor drily. Tegan stared angrily about her. The Doctor certainly had a point, and it didn't need all these nasty-looking home-made guns and Brazen shouting 'Go on – move yourself' to bring it home to her. In that quiet, reassuring tone of his that was not always as reliable as it sounded, the Doctor added, 'We'd better do as they say. We're quite safe as long as we keep calm.'

'Oh, all right,' she said sulkily, letting herself be bustled through the crowd in the wake of Mr Range. 'Of all the wretched, disorganised, chaotic planets I've ever seen, this is rock solid bottom. . . .'

As soon as she had stomped off accompanied by some of the Orderlies, Plantagenet brought the Doctor back to the question Norna had raised.

'The rocks beneath the soil? Well, yes . . . there is, as you've guessed, a rational explanation. . . .' The Doctor spoke with a confidence he did not feel. The immediate cause of the bombardment itself was hardly a problem to someone with the Doctor's training – although now was not the time for disclosures of that kind. But about the deeper 'why', he had only some dimly formed ideas, and there was a lot of

46

dangerous work to be done before they would be worth discussing. 'I'll know in time,' he said. 'If you let me investigate. On the other hand, if you're going to kill me, you'd better get on with it. I can't wait around all day for you.'

The stump-armed Orderly with the raised gun looked for a decision to Plantagenet, who glanced in turn at Brazen. But the big man's face was impassive – in matters of life and death the final word belonged to the leader.

'Kill him,' said Plantagenet after a moment. With a nod in the direction of the Doctor's would-be executioner he turned abruptly and walked away.

The Orderly shifted his crippled arm to bring the Doctor's head into his sights. But before his finger could tighten on the trigger Norna had grabbed the gun and was grappling with him. Hands reached out to pull her away. Turlough looked about for a weapon – anything – to fight them off. He grabbed at the hat-stand, trying to tug it out of the rubble.

The Orderlies had just managed to prise Norna away from the gun, giving the stump-armed gun-bearer the chance to aim again, when a remarkable thing happened. Yielding to Turlough's desperate efforts the hat-stand suddenly jerked loose from the rubble, and an enormous ball of light whooshed from it.

Turlough stopped dead, standing with the hat-stand raised, as astonished as anybody. The Doctor hurried to his side, fascinated at the phenomenon, and quite oblivious to the fact that the crowd around him had drawn back in terror. 'Like ball lightning,' he said. 'Must be residual energy from the TARDIS. Now that's very interesting . . .'

While the Doctor's mind scooted off to high planes of abstraction, Plantagenet fought hard to regain his composure. Even the unimaginative Brazen seemed shaken. There seemed to be no doubt that the Doctor had brought with him a device capable of terrible destruction, perhaps even of bringing down the bombardment.

*

The Orderlies that Brazen had set to watch Tegan and Mr Range had positioned themselves on the steps of the medical shelter, blocking the exit. Not that Tegan had any thoughts of escaping: with no TARDIS to run to, the medical shelter seemed the safest place on this unlucky planet.

Mr Range had given her the job of wiring up the phosphor lamps according to the Doctor's plan, and she was now sitting in Mr Range's little office behind the hydrazine steam engine cutting up lengths of cable. At the small desk one of the paramedics was unpacking more of the dangerous phosphor lamps from a storage crate, and she wondered if all this effort going into improving the illumination might not be better spent. On organising transport to a friendlier planet perhaps. Except that the depressingly low level of the technology on Frontios seemed to preclude any ideas of that kind.

She took a break to stretch her legs. Mr Range was showing one of his paramedics how to remove the electrodes from the acid jar. 'We're replacing the acid,' the little scientist explained. 'A completely fresh charge is needed, according to the Doctor's calculations.'

'The Doctor should be down here, helping us,' said Tegan. 'You people are totally irrational.'

'*They* are,' replied Mr Range mildly. 'I try to distance myself from their politics. Er . . . acid up to about here . . .' The paramedic was uncorking a large container of some oily fuming liquid. Mr Range carefully wiped down the electrodes and began connecting them up to the wire.

'This battery had better work,' said Tegan, thinking of all the efforts that had gone into getting it. But their dangerous adventure in the colony-ship seemed like a game compared with the new turn events had taken. The TARDIS destroyed! She still couldn't take it in. To be marooned forever on a planet whose only energy source was a glass bottle and some wires! And with the sinister young Plantagenet giving the orders!

'That was all play-acting out there, I hope?' asked Tegan, struck by a sudden thought. It was hard to understand why anyone should want to kill the Doctor, although she now knew many who had tried.

Mr Range pushed his glasses onto the bridge of his nose. 'Death is a daily occurrence on this planet. As you can see. This constant state of panic . . . the growing number of Rets. . . .' He explained to her about the Retrogrades, more of whom were deserting every day to hunt out in the wastes like animals.

'The Orderlies really shoot deserters?' asked Tegan.

'If they have to. A waste of life, but discipline is paramount.'

'Discipline!' She certainly wasn't going to stand by while they shot the Doctor. 'Every death increases the danger of extinction!'

'You think I'm not aware of that?' Mr Range called after her, as she swept off in the direction of the steps.

But she had only gone a few paces when she was brought to an abrupt halt. A hand, reaching up from one of the beds, had fastened around her own.

Tegan spun round. The wasted figure on the bed seemed so frail, but in spite of his deadly pallor and evident nearness to death – or perhaps because of it – his fingers held her in a steely grip. He was trying to speak, his mouth forming words that his dry throat could not give voice to. But she sensed the urgency of his plea for help. Her heart pounding, she took his other hand and leaned over him.

'Water,' she said efficiently to the paramedic tending to the acid jar. 'He needs some water.'

It had taken Turlough a little time to realise that the colonists regarded the Doctor's hat-stand as some sort of formidable weapon. Since the initial impressive pyrotechnics there had been no more unhat-standlike behaviour from it, but he continued to hold it at a casual angle intended to suggest that at any moment its terrifying virtuosity might be brought into play again.

The sense of danger that the innocent item of furniture generated had stirred Plantagenet to a new level of declamation. The Doctor listened patiently to a lengthy speech about the colonists of Frontios being at last face to face with their persecutors, and then said quietly, 'I'd like to know more about this precious rocks under the soil business myself. After all, whatever's going on here has put paid to my TARDIS.'

'You deny making war on us?' Plantagenet asked, staring defiantly at the hat-stand.

'If war it actually be,' said the Doctor enigmatically. 'You and I, Plantagenet, are stuck in the same shell-hole.' He weighed one of the missile fragments in his hand. 'Does anybody actually know where these are coming from?'

Norna offered Captain Revere's official explanation. 'One of the planets in the Veruna system.' And Brazen added, 'Without instruments we can't ascertain which one.'

'This rock analysis thing?' the Doctor muttered, pacing up and down. 'You've been looking into the whyfores. I think we should investigate the where froms.' He stopped in front of Plantagenet. 'Mr Range tells me you have a research room.'

It was Brazen who replied. 'The research facilities have been sequestrated on the dying orders of the late Captain.' The Doctor had already heard something about the accident: he gathered that a distillation vessel had exploded while Captain Revere was working in the research room.

'Yes, Mr Range told me. Funny, that.'

'You find my father's death amusing, Doctor?'

'Funny peculiar,' replied the Doctor without apology. 'For an experienced researcher to have that sort of bad luck. It wasn't as though he was handling the vessel at the time. . . .'

'How do you know that?' asked Norna.

'The face was burned beyond recognition, I think Mr Range said – but the hands were quite untouched.' As the Doctor spoke he was watching Brazen carefully, but the Chief Orderly replied without batting an eyelid, 'I don't think, Doctor, the research room falls within your remit.'

'But it's still got some useful stuff in it,' said Turlough, and then had to explain about their adventures in getting the acid jar. The Doctor shook his head. 'My dear Turlough, if these people don't want us inside, I don't see how . . .'

But Turlough knew how to change their minds. He raised the hat-stand and pointed it directly at Plantagenet. 'I think they'll let us have a look, Doctor.'

Mr Range covered the face of the wasted figure in the bed and turned to Tegan. 'Thank you. You can get back to your work now.' He began to make notes on his clipboard.

Tegan made her way back to the office with an empty feeling. She was certain the man had grabbed her hand to tell her something, but what she would never know. The paramedic working on the acid jar had left it to help the others disconnect the drip and make the bed ready for another of the wounded. She noticed that the new acid in the untended jar was beginning to bubble up around the neck, but the danger did not register. She could only see those dry lips of the dying man mouthing again the same round, hollow shape, trying to form a word. It might have been 'ground' or 'down'. It meant nothing to her, and everything, it seemed, to him, for he had given his life trying to tell her.

She climbed up on the filing cabinet to reach the top of the steam engine, and began to connect the first wires to the interrupter circuit, following the diagram the Doctor had sketched. Mr Range came into the office and with a key on a chain at his belt unlocked the filing cabinet and slid open a drawer. Tegan glanced down and saw him scribbling hasty notes in a file. As he closed the folder she managed to glimpse its title: *Deaths: Accountable*. Suddenly there was a cry from the other side of the generator. From her high perch Tegan could see that the acid jar was bubbling over, its sticky, fuming contents trickling over the floor.

Mr Range rushed out of the office to tend to the crisis. Tegan clambered down and was about to follow when she noticed that the filing cabinet was still open. She stopped to pick up the file Mr Range had been updating, and as she did so the folder underneath it caught her eye. Its title was *Deaths: Unaccountable.*

There was no time to ponder on this odd discovery, for at that moment the interrupter she had been working on began to click, and all around the shelter the phosphor lamps up on the walls glowed brightly. Mr Range had got the Doctor's circuit working. Guiltily Tegan dropped the files back in the drawer and pushed it shut, expecting Mr Range to return at any moment. But when she peered round the corner of the generator she could see he was still busy mopping up the aftermath.

Her curiosity had got her into trouble before, but the temptation was irresistible. She tugged at the drawer . . . and was disappointed to discover it had locked automatically.

Sledgehammers smashed into the stones walling up the entrance to the research room. Turlough stood behind the Orderlies who wielded them, keeping Plantagenet and Brazen in his line of fire, almost beginning to believe in the imaginary powers of the threatening hat-stand himself. The Doctor too, whether play-acting or from simple absent-mindedness, seemed to have forgotten that the weapon Turlough held was only their familiar piece of furniture from the TARDIS console room, for at one point when it swept round in his direction he pulled Norna gingerly out of the way with a muttered 'Careful with that thing.'

As the last few sledgehammer blows were struck Plantagenet exchanged a glance with Brazen. The Chief Orderly knew what was in his leader's mind and shook his head in a slight gesture unseen by the others. The unknown power of the device Turlough held was too dangerous, and they should bide their time.

The Doctor was the first to enter through the ragged gap. The Orderlies laid down their heavy tools and respectfully stepped aside for him, but in the movement neither the Doctor nor Turlough noticed Plantagenet surreptitiously pick up one of the sledgehammers.

'Well, here we are,' said the Doctor, unashamedly stating the obvious as he surveyed the few items of equipment that remained. 'There's enough here to keep us busy.' He turned to Turlough. 'You can help. I want to run a series on halides and silica.'

'What?' asked Turlough. The Doctor often made the mistake of assuming everyone else was as clever as he was. But Norna was already at his side, jotting down notes. 'I'll help,' she said. 'It's quite easy.'

The Doctor emptied out his pockets, spilling several of the small, hard stone-like objects onto the workbench. As Norna picked one up she caught a sudden movement out of the corner of her eye and spun round. 'Look out!'

Plantagenet had raised the sledgehammer above his head and was about to bring it down on Turlough's head. Hearing Norna's cry the Doctor's young companion jumped back and swung the hat-stand round, pointing it directly at Plantagenet.

Terrified of what he imagined to be advanced alien technology, the young leader stumbled back, dropping the sledgehammer. 'No . . . please!' What happened next was extraordinary, at least to those present who had travelled in the TARDIS and knew the hat-stand of old as a harmless, somewhat unnecessary encumbrance of the console room. There was no ball of light, not even sparks. But Plantagenet, standing directly in its line of fire, suddenly gave a moan of pain and crumpled to the floor.

Brazen was the first to recover, and reached for the fallen sledgehammer. Still shocked at the sight of Plantagenet lifeless on the floor, Turlough turned the hat-stand on the Chief Orderly. Brazen hesitated for a moment, then threw down the weapon.

'This joke's gone far enough.' It was the Doctor who spoke, striding across to Turlough. He grabbed the hat-stand from him and set it upright in its proper position. Then as part of the same decisive movement he peeled off his cream-coloured cricketing coat, hung it on one of the pegs and knelt down to put his ear to Plantagenet's chest.

'Delayed effect of a glancing blow,' he pronounced after a moment. As the Doctor straightened up Turlough glimpsed the young leader's chest under the shirt the Doctor had pulled upon. He saw a terrible dark bruise over the heart. 'He's been hit by one of the last wave of missiles,' the Doctor confirmed, and waved a hand to Turlough and Norna. 'Stay here. Set up those tests.'

The Doctor was about to lift up the limp body when Brazen intervened and took Plantagenet from him. Gathering the young leader in his huge arms, Brazen hurried out after the Doctor.

5

Downwardness

'Oh, rabbits!' exclaimed Tegan, looking round for something to open the locked filing cabinet. On the table were some thin knives of the kind she had seen used by the paramedics for surgery. Tegan took the most robust-looking one she could find, and was scraping it around inside the lock when suddenly a hand clamped around her wrist.

'What do you think you're doing?' The voice belonged to Mr Range. His fingers were surprisingly strong, and she couldn't stop him prising the scalpel from her hand. 'I . . . I'm trying to get the drawer open, if you really want to know,' she said, trying not to sound afraid. The little scientist was pressing her back against the filing cabinet, and the scalpel was now pointing at her stomach. 'Curiosity is dangerous on Frontios,' he said in a low voice.

'Not as dangerous as ignorance,' said Tegan. Mr Range's eyes narrowed behind the round glasses. 'You know something. What have you seen?' Around the corner of the hydrazine steam generator Tegan could see the bottom of the steps that led up to the door. The armed Orderly delegated to guard them was sitting there with his back to them. She wondered if the fear she sensed in the scientist's voice was due to this official presence. Perhaps after all there was something in the allegations that Mr Range was a traitor?

'How about "unaccountable deaths"?' she suggested,

keeping her voice down. Mr Range paled. 'Forget you ever saw the file,' he whispered, glancing back towards the armed Orderly. Reassured by his evident unease, Tegan began to reassert herself. 'There's something going on here, isn't there? Some racket you're into.'

Mr Range gestured nervously, bringing the scalpel within inches of her face. Uncertain whether he was distraught or deliberately threatening her, Tegan jerked her hand out of his grasp and headed for the steps. But the Orderly she expected to find there had already risen to his feet and was striding up the steps towards the open door.

She looked up to see the Doctor hurrying down towards her. Behind him was Brazen, carrying the inert body of the young leader. 'Those wires – quick,' said the Doctor, waving a hand towards the recently installed phosphor lamps. 'Rip them down. Now!' Mr Range emerged from the office to see what the interruption was, and Tegan was relieved to see that he had put down the scalpel. The Doctor flicked his fingers towards the scientist. 'Damp cloths. Anything damp.'

Tegan helped Brazen lay the pale, inert body out on the bed recently vacated by the other unfortunate colonist. 'What's the matter with him?' she asked. 'Fibrillating,' said the Doctor tersely, carefully folding the damp cloths Mr Range had brought, and laying them across Plantagenet's chest. 'It's his heart,' Mr Range explained, the recent incident in the office apparently forgotten. 'The Doctor's going to get it going again.'

With a muttered order the Doctor waved Mr Range away in the direction of the acid jar. The wires the Doctor held led to the now silent interrupter of the hydrazine steam engine, and from there to the acid jar where Mr Range was now standing ready to make the connection.

The Doctor knelt over the young ruler, pressing the ends of the wires into the cloth pads. 'Are we ready, Mr Range? Right, give me some current . . . now!'

Mr Range closed the circuit. The interrupter began clicking slowly and the pale form on the bed stiffened. 'Let the voltage build,' shouted the Doctor, jerking the wires away from the improvised pads in a flurry of sparks. The clicking from the generator became more rapid, and the Doctor plunged the wires back into position. There was a sizzling sound, Plantagenet's eyes opened wide and his whole body became rigid, arching up off the bed with a suddenness that threw the Doctor off balance.

'Stop it!' shouted the Doctor. 'Disconnect!'

The clicking stopped abruptly. With a great sigh that sounded like his last, Plantagenet sank back onto the dishevelled sheets and lay still. Brazen confronted the Doctor across the bed, and said in an awed whisper. 'You've killed him.'

The Doctor drew the blanket over Plantagenet's chest. 'It was certainly touch and go for a moment,' he said. As he stepped back Tegan could see the blanket slowly rise and fall with the rhythm of healthy breathing. The thin young figure in the bed would be luckier than the former occupant.

Norna was busy assembling distillation equipment on the bench. Turlough was helping in a distracted way, hunting out the various components she needed. But he insisted on talking while she was trying to concentrate. 'I wouldn't put up with it. All this having to improvise, and making do, and food rationing, and getting showered by these deadly things. What's the point?'

'We don't have the technology to go anywhere else. Or hadn't you noticed?'

Turlough cast a wistful glance at the hat-stand where the Doctor's coat still hung, an inescapable reminder of the TARDIS. 'I'm beginning to know the feeling,' he sighed, and ambled off to fetch a clamp. When he came back he continued, as if he'd been giving the problem a lot of thought. 'Why didn't you dig deep bunkers? The Arar-Jecks of Heiradi hollowed out a huge subterranean city under their planet during the 20 aeon war.'

'There was a quarry where the stone came from to build the medical shelter. They converted it into a place to get away from the bombardment. When I was very small we always used to go to the quarry when the bombardments came. And then all that got stopped.'

'Stopped?' echoed Turlough. 'Why?'

Norna tightened the clamp. The inelegant construction on the bench was almost complete. 'Captain Revere made a law against it.'

As far as Turlough was concerned laws didn't explain anything. 'A law against what?' Norna was concentrating on unscrewing one of the phosphor lamps. 'Forbidding any digging in the ground . . .'

'There must have been a reason?' Turlough said. But he wasn't sure – even allowing for their extraordinarily unpleasant environment, the colonists of Frontios seemed to be running their planet on very eccentric lines.

Norna shook her head. 'Captain Revere never gave reasons.' Turlough noticed her reaching into the phosphor lamp with a spatula and carefully removing a few drops of the sticky substance inside, an action that confirmed his view that these people must be crazy – or at least that they had developed a very unhealthy relationship with danger.

He stepped forward to stop her, but she laughed at him and showed him how to use the drops of phosphor to light a fire. The little pile of chippings under the retort burst into flames, and they watched it for a moment warming the liquid in the bottom of the vessel. Then she suddenly said, 'Except once . . . He gave me a reason once. I was little, sitting on his knee in the State Room. I asked why we couldn't go below the ground any more. He said . . .' She frowned, trying to bring back the memory. 'It was a child's answer . . . It seemed quite sensible at the time.'

'What did he say?' prompted Turlough.

'He said . . . Yes, that was it . . .' The liquid in the retort began to bubble, turning from yellow to a darkish green. 'He said the earth was . . . hungry.'

Turlough helped Norna crush some of the small stones in an improvised vice and dissolve the powder in warm acid. She selected some of the stones to be held against a kind of primitive grindstone and polished flat before etching them with acid and inspecting the result through a large magnifying glass. Norna made careful notes of everything she did, but it was all a mystery to Turlough, and his attention kept straying around the room, particularly to the mineral samples on the shelves.

She noticed his inattention when he handed her a flask instead of the pressure filter she had asked for. 'Sorry . . .' he said, 'I was just wondering . . . these rocks.'

'What about them?'

'They're all labelled. With dates. They must have come from somewhere.'

'They did – the quarry.' Norna raised her head from her notes and saw that Turlough had jumped up on top of one of the larger cabinets and was reaching up towards the overhead beam. 'The dates are recent,' he called back to her as he climbed. 'According to you the quarry's been closed for years. . . .'

From the beam it was an easy climb to the hatch in the ceiling through which they had first entered the research room. The block and tackle was still hanging over the side of the hull where they had left it. Turlough began to haul it in and lower it towards the research room floor.

'They obviously didn't install this just for us,' he said, shinning down the rope.

'It's for lifting equipment,' said Norna, trying to conceal her irritation at his playfulness when there was so much work to be done.

'What equipment?' asked Turlough. 'What's so heavy down there that needs a pulley and tackle?'

If Norna had stopped to think she would have realised that it was quite a good question. But she was busy making notes as she checked the missile samples, so all she said was, 'Very ingenious.'

She didn't speak again until he asked her a direct question. 'How long ago were you actually in this research room?' He had lowered the hook, and was pulling the block and tackle along the overhead beam, scanning the floor beneath it.

'When I was small. I came here with my father when he was still Captain Revere's personal Science Assistant.'

'Was this block and tackle here then?' Turlough asked. Norna put down her notes, suddenly realising what Turlough was getting at. There was no block and tackle in the research room as she remembered it, which meant that some time since, Captain Revere had ordered it to be installed specially. But specially for what?

'Of course,' she said. 'These floor plates are solid metal. Heavy solid metal.' But even as she spoke, Turlough had already found what he was looking for. He pulled a large metal plug out of the floor, revealing a ring bolted into the panel. 'The hook goes in here,' he said excitedly, dragging the block and tackle down towards the ring. 'I think we're about to find out where Captain Revere got his rock collection.'

Plantagenet stirred and looked up at the Doctor and Tegan. 'Try to get some rest,' said the Doctor, but his voice did not soothe the young leader. 'Rest? Death is the only rest you bring to Frontios.' The attempt to speak brought back the searing pain in his chest as he struggled to sit up.

Brazen leaned forward over him. 'Don't exert yourself, Leader. We're in control of the situation.' Plantagenet was glad to see a face he could trust. He reached up and took the big man's hand. 'I have responsibilities,' he said in a voice that was barely a whisper. 'Frontios depends on me.'

'Yes, it certainly needs a strong leader,' said the Doctor with a smile. He mopped Plantagenet's forehead with a damp cloth while Tegan held his head. Brazen patted the hand that held his. 'I'd advise adopting the Doctor's strategy, Leader. The man seems to know what he's about.'

'You've changed your mind about him?' A trace of panic flitted across the young leader's face. Brazen paused for a breath, looking hard in the Doctor's direction. 'I'm reserving judgement about that. But there's no escaping the fact that he saved your life.'

With an effort of will Plantagenet lifted himself on his elbows to peer closely at the Doctor. 'Saved my life? Is this true?'

The Doctor winked. 'Not a word to the Time Lords.'

Tegan changed the dressing on Plantagenet's chest, and one of the Orderlies brought a bowl of hot soup. Soon the young leader was well enough to lie propped up on pillows, and while Mr Range was in the office undergoing some further questioning from the still suspicious Chief Orderly, the Doctor seized the opportunity of a quiet conversation with Plantagenet. There was much that he needed to know, but he realised he had to be careful not to arouse hostility again.

'I can see that Frontios isn't the easiest planet to rule,' the Doctor conceded, after he had heard a little of their history.

'Thirty years of bombardments, Doctor,' said Plantagenet. 'Were it not for my father, this colony would have despaired itself into extinction long ago.'

'Yes,' said the Doctor thoughtfully. 'Bit of a problem keeping up the impetus, I bet.'

Tegan came back to the bedside, plumping up a clean pillow to go under Plantagenet's head. 'Your bloke Brazen doesn't trust us an inch,' she couldn't resist observing. A trace of something that might have been a smile softened Plantagenet's thin lips. 'He's a good man. If rather narrow in his outlook.'

'He's planning to move you to the State Room.' Tegan had overheard him talking to Mr Range in the office. She was not prepared for the effect the news had on Plantagenet. 'The State Room!' he exclaimed. 'No, I must stay here, with my people.'

'The democratic touch, eh?' said the Doctor.

Plantagenet's eyes narrowed. 'Hardly democracy, Doctor. I must remain in public sight. If for one moment the Colonists of Frontios think I am dead . . . there will be anarchy.'

The block and tackle creaked under the weight as Turlough and Norna strained together on the rope. 'You're sure this is meant to lift?' asked Norna between clenched teeth. Turlough had already begun to doubt his own theory, and was wondering now whether perhaps the ring in the floor was meant to tie something down rather than lift something up. But that didn't explain the block and tackle. 'One more go,' he said. 'Come on . . . heave!'

His doubts evaporated as a dark crack appeared in the metal plating beneath their feet. Slowly the whole section of flooring lifted up on a hinge, revealing a rectangle of blackness. While Turlough tied off the tackle, Norna directed the light of her phosphor lamp into the hole. 'The secret excavation area!' she said under her breath. Where Captain Revere had continued his own subterranean investigations, long after he had forbidden others from going underground.

Turlough insisted on going down first. Norna lit his way as he went hand over hand down the rough ladder, and then passed down the lamp and followed him. 'Careful,' said Turlough's voice from the darkness. 'It's a bit crumbly in here.'

As her eyes adjusted to the gloom, she looked round to find herself in a shallow pit with walls that trickled with little rivulets of silt. In places the rock had been propped up with metal plates and tubing borrowed from the colony ship, but the supports were all buckled.

Turlough was inspecting the walls. 'This rock's . . . sort of moth-eaten.' He tapped it, and a small hole appeared under his fist.

'Look out!' cried Norna, jumping back as the wall burst open in a sudden rush of debris. The miniature landslide was more frightening than dangerous, but it covered them with dust and made it difficult to breathe in the confined space.

'We'd better go back,' said Turlough, clutching his handkerchief to his mouth.

'No, wait!' said Norna, taking the lamp from him and directing it into the space revealed by the shifting rock. The beam reflected on the walls of a long tunnel disappearing into the distance. 'Look, there's a way through. In the gloomy glow of the phosphor lamp she noticed a curiously distant expression in Turlough's eyes. 'Don't tell me you're frightened.'

Turlough shook his head, and moved slowly forward into the tunnel, drawn by a strange fascination. 'No, it's just . . . like something I remember . . .' Norna followed, the phosphor lamp she held making his shadow dance ahead, as if they were following some great restless creature of the rocks.

In the medical shelter, the Doctor was explaining the simple physics of the situation to Plantagenet. 'And what's making you so vulnerable to attack is the thin atmosphere on Frontios.'

The pale young man in the bed seemed curiously resistant to scientific explanation, but the Doctor had at least managed to arouse his curiosity. 'But why do they come so frequently now?'

The Doctor got up from the bed. 'I have some theories about that. And with your permission I'll go back to the research room and confirm them.'

Plantagenet sank back on the pillow. His eyes, though still

bright with interest, lay deep in their sockets, and he was clearly in need of sleep. 'Thank you, Doctor.' He gestured towards Tegan. 'Your assistant may stay here with me. Then we'll all trust one another.'

The Doctor accepted the somewhat imperious command with good grace, and when Tegan bristled with resistance he shot her a stern glance that warned her not to make trouble. He turned to Mr Range. 'Then perhaps you'll come with me?' Brazen seemed about to protest, so the Doctor quickly extended the invitation to him. 'Everybody can help, Chief Orderly. Come and muck in.'

'My duty is here with the Leader,' Brazen replied heavily.

The Doctor took Mr Range by the arm and made for the steps. 'Good. Then we'll see you later.'

As they disappeared, Brazen beckoned to one of the Orderlies. 'Keep an eye on them,' he said in a low voice. 'Just for the sake of security.'

Tegan helped the paramedics restore the lighting, and once the interrupter was clicking like a giant cricket on top of the steam generator, and the lighting had reached a more cheerful level, she found herself standing by Plantagenet's bed. The pale, sleeping face looked almost peaceful now. All around her she could hear the restless, painful sounds of the injured, and they seemed like a commentary on her own thoughts. In her mind's eye she could still see the drawn face of the man who had died in that bed, mouthing some word she would never understand. She wondered if there was a connection with the mysterious folders in Mr Range's office, and the threat of invasion that hung over the planet.

She was startled to find Brazen standing beside her. He was disconcertingly silent for several moments, gazing down at the sleeping leader. Then, in a surprisingly gentle voice he said, 'He'll fill out – find his strength. I watched his father grow the same. The odds were terrible against the Captain, but he held this Colony together with a will of steel.'

This new facet of Brazen moved Tegan to attempt some

civilised conversation. 'I'm beginning to see the problems of this planet,' she began, and then found herself stuck for words. 'I mean, with so many deaths . . . accountable and unaccountable . . .'

The moment the words were out of her mouth she knew she had made a blunder. Brazen turned on her. 'What do you know about unaccountable deaths?' Tegan shrugged. 'Just a phrase I came across.' He grabbed her arm and pulled her face close to his, speaking in a low tone to avoid disturbing Plantagenet. 'Came across where?'

Tegan thought it best not to struggle. 'I don't know . . . Maybe I heard it.' But the Chief Orderly was not going to be satisfied with vague answers. 'Or saw it in some records . . .' he suggested.

Tegan straightened up. There was no point in covering up for Mr Range if Brazen knew about the folders. 'Yes, I saw inside the filing cabinet. I was only—'

The Chief Orderly let go of her arm. From the look of triumph in his face Tegan realised she had made her second big blunder. 'Filing cabinet?' he crowed. 'Show me.' And he marched Tegan round the hydrazine steam generator into the little office.

'You know, Mr Range,' said the Doctor as they marched through the colony-ship corridors towards the research centre, 'if I'm right, these so-called missiles of yours are nothing more nor less than natural meteorites.'

'Meteorites? In such quantities?'

'Unusual, I grant you,' the Doctor conceded. 'I'm working on the theory that one of the Veruna planets may have disintegrated.'

'And we're right in the path, eh?' said Mr Range. 'But if it's a sort of asteroid belt, surely Captain Revere would have detected it?'

They had reached the door of the research room. Before going in, the Doctor paused to examine a broken control panel in the corridor. Apologetically he said, 'I think he did detect it, Mr Range.' And then, with one of those infuriating grasshopper jumps of thought that made his conversations so hard to follow, he said, 'What puzzles me is how this ship managed to crash in the first place. With all this autonomous guidance.'

'The systems failed,' said Mr Range patiently. He had explained it all once before to the Doctor.

'Let me get this straight,' said the Doctor, propping himself up against the corridor wall. 'The systems failed *before* the crash?'

'Without the failure there would have been no crash, Doctor. The guidance systems . . . everything . . . all went together!' Mr Range didn't entirely see the relevance of this train of thought, and gently mentioned the fact. The Doctor began rather ponderously to muster the evidence, counting off the items on his fingers. 'Colony-ships, Mr Range . . . Possible meteorites . . . Talk of precious stones beneath the soil. Don't you detect a distinct *downwardness* in all this?'

And with that sobering thought he followed Mr Range into the research room.

Plantagenet stirred on the bed, his sleep disturbed perhaps by the shrill tones of Tegan's voice from the office as she tried to talk herself out of her predicament. 'I could be wrong. Maybe I read it in a book somewhere. *Deaths Unaccountable* – I think that was the title.' A little later her voice rose to a higher pitch of protestation: 'Hey, you can't do that to Mr Range's medical records!'

None of these sounds wakened Plantagenet, not even the noise of Brazen battering on the filing cabinet with some blunt instrument. Sleep seemed to be soaking into him, so that his jaw sagged open and the muscles of his face sank into shapelessness. One hand twitched and slipped down the gap between the bed and the wall, dropping to the floor as if some unseen force were plucking at it.

It was the sense of something pulling at his arm that woke him to drowsy consciousness. As he tried to sit up he rolled against the wall and the blanket slipped from the bed. He found himself following it, the top half of his body sliding over the edge of the mattress and thudding onto the flagstone floor as the bed shifted away from the wall. He squinted sideways and saw that his hand was now somehow embedded in the stone, which had begun to break up into a curious texture of small wormholes. He tried to call for help, but the muscles of his mouth had given up all their energy to the relentless downward force that was taking him prisoner.

Brazen's assault on the filing cabinet became louder, accompanied by soldierly curses and continued protestations from Tegan. Then, with a screech of twisted metal, it came open. Brazen began flicking through the files. 'So, it's Mr Range who's been spreading these rumours . . .'

'What rumours?' asked Tegan, getting her breath back after all the shouting.

'Disinformation about the status quo.' Brazen emerged from the office snapping his fingers to one of the Orderlies. 'Keep an eye on things down here.' He ran up the steps with the file to confer with the Orderly guarding the door.

As Tegan watched him go her eye fell on Plantagenet's bed. She caught her breath – it was empty! She ran to it and found him struggling weakly in the gap between the bed and the wall. The flagstones around him were now pitted with wormholes, and his body was rapidly sinking into them as though the solid stone were a viscous liquid.

Tegan screamed, terrified as much by the silent agony in the young ruler's eyes as the incongruous horror of the scene. She saw him try to cry out too, but only a faint choking sound came from his white lips. She reached out for him, bending over him, scrabbling at his loose garments, but they came away like flakes of moth-wings in her hands.

She couldn't hold him. In front of her eyes the earth sucked him down, draining his physical shape away through the strange worm-holes. . . . And then there was the sound of running feet, and a crush of Orderlies and paramedics closing in, and the arms of the big Chief Orderly supporting her from falling as the medical shelter reeled around her.

6

Beneath the Rocks

Mr Range hurried across the research room to the edge of
the open pit. 'They've gone!' The Doctor nodded, sur-
veying the workbench where Norna had set up the
equipment. 'Exploring, by the look of it. Turlough's a
restless sort of chap. But I see they've completed the rock
analysis.' He picked up a test tube and, taking a magnifying
glass from his coat pocket, subjected it to careful scrutiny.

It was a polished section of missile fragment, immersed in
a pale liquid. 'They look very like Widmanstatten patterns
to me . . . Which would seem to confirm . . . What's the
problem, Mr Range?'

The little scientist was hovering by the edge of the
excavation area, looking anxiously down into blackness.
'I'm afraid they may be in danger down there.'

'Hardly,' said the Doctor. 'Turlough wouldn't risk an
unsafe tunnel.'

Mr Range shook his head. 'No, not that. I've suspected
for a long time that Captain Revere ordered the quarry
closed because of something he found.'

The Doctor slowly put down the test-tube. 'What sort
of . . . something?'

'A geological feature, perhaps. Something beneath the
surface it might be dangerous to disturb.'

*

The sombre glow of the phosphor lamp steered Norna and Turlough deeper into the tunnel, a small bubble of light that unfolded foot after foot of darkness in front of them, and let it close again behind them as they went. Then the reflections seemed to shine brighter from the rocks around them, as if the bubble had grown in size. Turlough assumed this was because their eyes were now fully accustomed to the gloom, but Norna stopped abruptly and ran to touch the walls.

'Hold the light still a minute . . . Yes . . .'

'What is it?' Turlough asked, raising the lamp. He was surprised to find his hand shaking slightly.

'The walls – have you noticed? They're quite different here.'

They were smooth, almost as if they had been polished. Turlough stood beside Norna, staring into the black rock. Distorted reflections of themselves returned their gaze, like phantom prisoners beneath the glassy surface. 'We ought to be getting back,' Turlough said flatly.

'In a minute. I want to see where this leads to.' She walked a little way on, leaving Turlough touching the walls. They reminded him of something. A deep buried memory began to stir.

Norna was amused at his timorousness. 'Come on, chicken-feet. Bring the torch. The tunnel opens out at the end here.'

Turlough attempted a laugh. 'I'm not frightened. Just thinking responsibly.'

'I'll leave you to it then,' said Norna. 'I'm going on.'

'In the dark? You can't. No, wait. I'm coming . . .'

Quite suddenly the walls opened out. Reflecting back from the curved rock that enveloped them, their single lamp was multiplied to many, and there was more than enough light to see across to the other side of the cave.

On their way they had come across boulders, but here was something larger: several silver spheres were positioned about the cave, as if they had stumbled across a giant game of bowls. 'That's funny,' said Norna, pausing to examine their strange carved markings.

Turlough stopped in the middle of the cave. 'Can we go back now? Please?' He looked so absurdly vulnerable with the lamp above his head that she couldn't resist laughing. But the echo turned the sound to unintended mockery, and this was too much of a challenge for Turlough. He marched across the cave towards the tunnel in the opposite wall. 'Come on, then. I'm only thinking of you. If you get lost I'm not coming looking for you.'

He disappeared into the tunnel, and the darkness closed in around the cave like a black-gloved fist. 'Hey, wait for me,' Norna called out, and ran after him.

The faint glow of the receding lamp seemed to strike life into the silver spheres. But it was more than the appearance of movement, these shifting shards of light on the exotic markings. Slowly one of the spheres began to unroll . . . With the gait of a huge silver woodlouse it started to move, following the firefly of the phosphor lamp that flitted away down the tunnel.

Mr Range had managed to root out a crate of twelve lamps, each individually wrapped in fire-proof cloth. He unpacked one and carefully turned it upside down once or twice until the glow developed. He passed it to the Doctor, who was halfway down the ladder. 'Are you sure, Doctor? I want to help.'

The Doctor's voice echoed back from the excavation area. 'You will, Mr Range. By staying here. These sort of adventures depend on a well-manned home base.'

The Orderlies pulled the bed away from the wall. 'Is this where you say it happened?' asked Brazen. Very shaken, Tegan nodded. 'As if something were sucking him through the floor. I must get the Doctor . . .'

Brazen's grip on her arm tightened. 'I don't think so. We're going to need you here.' But at that moment the door at the top of the steps burst open. Orderlies ran to block the way, as a crowd of colonists tried to push and shove their way in. Tegan saw several cudgels among the angrily waving arms, and recognised the face of Cockerill at the head of them.

'What's the meaning of this crass behaviour?' boomed Brazen, mounting the steps. 'You – Cockerill – what's going on?'

'Just trying to control the crowd, sir. There's unrest about our leader.'

Muttering among themselves the crowd slowly edged out of the door as Brazen advanced. 'You're an Orderly, aren't you, Cockerill? Put a stop to it. That's the meaning of the word.' The murmuring grew, and Tegan, approaching the bottom of the steps for a better view, heard it develop into a chant: 'He's dead. The leader's dead.'

Brazen stepped out through the door and stood in front of it, glowering at Cockerill, as if the words were his. 'And you've come to show them he's alive, I suppose. What do you think this is, man? A waxwork museum?' He snatched a cudgel from one of the raised arms in the crowd and waved it above his head. 'There's some authentic Retrograde material among this crowd, I can see. Get back to your business and leave Plantagenet and myself to get on with ours.' Brazen stood in the doorway for a moment, watching the subdued crowd begin to break up. Then he threw the weapon contemptuously to the ground, turned on his heels and went back inside.

What she had seen of this from the bottom of the stairs made Tegan miss the Doctor more than ever. Frontios seemed so hopeless without him. As she mounted the steps she noticed that one of the paramedics had even managed to make a mess of setting up the lamps. The wiring that ran along the wall at that point was loosely twisted together –

very likely to cause the system to fuse and undo all their hard work. That settled it, as far as she was concerned. While Brazen was still outside dealing with the crowd, Tegan made for the top of the steps. As these Frontios people did everything so badly, escaping shouldn't be too difficult.

She was wrong. She was halfway up the steps when one of the Orderlies behind her shouted a warning, and several pairs of feet came running towards her. She leant over the handrail with the thought of vaulting down into the area below. But seeing the higgledy-piggledy collection of beds she decided that the unfortunate patients had suffered enough already without the indignity of being jumped on.

The lighting cables gave her an idea. She reached out and wrested them away from the wall, pulling them apart at the loosely twisted join. The lighting immediately dimmed. Holding a cable end in each hand she advanced down the steps towards the Orderlies who were coming for her. 'Get back,' she cried. 'This is dangerous!'

'Put them down!' boomed a voice from the steps above. She spun round to find Brazen bearing down on her. The rectangle of daylight that shone through the open door behind him looked very inviting – and very distant. 'We'll have none of that sort of activity. Come on, drop it.'

She held the wires tightly as he advanced. She hoped that looking determined would stop him, because she didn't believe for a moment that she'd be capable of electrocuting him. Brazen seemed to have arrived at the same judgement himself, because he continued to close in on her.

And then, just as he reached out to wrap his big hands around her fists, she jammed the two ends of the wire together. There was a blinding explosion of sparks, a loud noise like a motor bike backfiring . . . and the lights died completely.

Tegan put her head down and ran for the top of the steps towards the welcoming patch of daylight. She heard Brazen thundering out behind her, 'She's getting away . . . Stop her.' But in the darkness and confusion nobody did.

She slammed the door shut and hung tightly to the ringed handle, looking for something to wedge it with. She could already hear heavy footsteps ascending the steps – at any moment the door would be yanked open and she would be a prisoner again. And then she saw the cudgel.

She grabbed it and jammed it through the ring. At that very moment somebody took hold of the handle on the other side and tried to turn it. The cudgel jammed tighter in the ring, and the door held. Without waiting any longer Tegan ran off in the direction of the colony-ship.

Turlough was still wrestling with the extraordinary feeling that he had seen all this – the black glassy rock and the winding tunnels – somewhere before. 'It's natural rock, you see,' he told Norna. 'That's the point. Natural rock, refined and polished.'

'It must have been somewhere you've visited. Maybe with the Doctor?' Norna suggested, hoping that sensible questions would help him keep hold of himself.

'Oh, I can't remember,' he replied airily. 'I've been everywhere. Everywhere that counts.' Norna smiled. 'Even Frontios,' she said. They turned a corner, and she took the lamp from him and walked a little more briskly.

But they hadn't gone far before Turlough stopped again, drawn once more to the reflections swimming in the dark, distorting mirror of the walls. 'Oh, come on,' said Norna, rather less patiently. 'Stop day-dreaming.'

'It's more like a nightmare,' Turlough replied slowly. 'It's as if I keep glimpsing something out of the corner of my eye.'

Norna stopped beside him. There was certainly something dark and mysterious about the deep shine of the walls – if you had time to stop and worry about things like that. 'Oh, come on,' she said. 'There's much more to see. . . .'

Reluctantly Turlough let her drag him away. They walked in silence for a moment, and then he said suddenly, 'And there's a word that goes with it. Tractators . . . that's it!'

'What?' said Norna.

'Tractators . . .' he repeated. 'I've no idea what it means.'

'Not "it" – "them",' said Norna, deciding to humour him. ' "Tractators" must be things in the plural.'

He nodded, then said slowly, 'Things . . . or beings of some kind. Yes . . . they breathe, I know that.' And he went on muttering the word "Tractators" until Norna was sick of it. She began to wonder if it wasn't after all time to turn back.

She didn't know then that there was no turning back. As their footsteps and the comfortable bubble of light moved off along the tunnel her ears failed to catch the slithering movement of the silvery creatures that pursued them, and she did not see in the darkness behind the faint white glow of their underbellies.

The Doctor was not very fond of tunnels at the best of times. They were frequently damp, dark, deep and dangerous, and as a method of transport ranked only a little higher than sitting absolutely still under water waiting for the right current. The best place to be in a tunnel was outside, and if you had to be inside, the less inside you were the better.

Despite these principles, acquired from long experience, the Doctor found himself once more not merely inside a tunnel, but trying to get further in with every step. And there was something about this particular tunnel that he didn't like at all. The smoothness of the walls, perhaps. The fact that though deep and dark it was not actually damp, as any self-respecting tunnel ought to be. Most of all, the odd phenomenon that he noticed when by way of experiment he hid his phosphor lamp under his coat to shut out the artificial light and come face to face with the tunnel in its natural state. The darkness was not complete!

He stopped to try it again, buttoning his coat to be doubly sure. This time instead of the very faint glow emanating evenly from all the walls, he noticed a distinct smear of light moving towards him from the direction he had come.

He ducked back into a niche in the wall. Footsteps were accompanying the light. And then he heard a familiar, somewhat uneasy voice. 'Doctor . . . Are you there?'

The Doctor unbuttoned his coat and stepped forward. 'I thought you were supposed to be guarding the rear, Mr Range?' The little scientist jumped at the appearance of the Doctor in a sudden bloom of light. 'It's my daughter, Doctor. I can't let you take all the risk.'

'Ah, well,' said the Doctor, taking this unhappy development philosophically. 'A risk shared is a risk doubled. Come on . . .'

Tegan slowed her pace as she approached the entrance to the colony-ship. She remembered the guards posted there, and was puzzled to find no sign of them. It wasn't until she got to the ramp that she saw them: two slumped bodies inside the double doors of the entrance.

A glimpse of movement inside the colony-ship made her jump down behind the cover of the line of crates. Several unkempt colonists emerged from the ship, carrying sacks and boxes. Tegan remembered what Brazen had said about the Rets. It looked as if the rumour about Plantagenet had sounded the signal for general looting.

She knew that the cudgel in the door handle wouldn't hold Brazen off for long and decided she couldn't wait until the Rets had disappeared from sight. In any case, they seemed more concerned with their loot than with her. She ran quickly up the ramp and slipped inside.

She found the big Causeway without much difficulty, coming across the bodies of several other security Orderlies on the way. When she got to the research room she was alarmed to find it deserted, and ran immediately to the edge of the excavation area and looked down into the uninviting darkness. 'Doctor! Hello, is anybody down there? Hey, Doctor!'

The Doctor raised his hand and signalled for quiet. 'I can't hear anything,' said Mr Range after a moment.

'Sssh . . . listen.' The Doctor had turned to face the way they had come. For a moment he thought he heard his name being called from a long way down the tunnel, but it may just have been the odd effect of the echoes. He shrugged, and was about to move on when an unmistakable sound froze his blood. It was a human scream, coming from somewhere in the tunnel directly ahead.

'I certainly heard that,' said Mr Range.

Echoing feet ran towards them. A distraught shape rushed towards them out of the darkness. Only when it was directly upon them did the Doctor recognise the terrified, fleeing figure. He caught hold of it, dragging it struggling to the ground. Mr Range held up his phosphor lamp and peered through his glasses at the petrifying fear on the face of Turlough. Wide-open eyes gazed back unseeingly at the lamp.

The Doctor held him firmly. 'Turlough! It's me, the Doctor.'

The young man's mouth opened, and the words came slowly, as if he were giving utterance for the first time in his life. 'Tractators . . . I've seen them.'

While the paramedics worked on the lighting system Tegan had so effectively fused, Brazen dealt with the urgent problem of opening the door. He signalled to four of his Orderlies to haul one of the beds up the steps to use as a battering ram. After slamming the end of the bed against the door several times it splintered, and at last burst open.

Once outside, Brazen picked two of his best men to accompany him on a quick recce of the settlement. It didn't take him long to come to the conclusions Tegan had reached. Looters had become a serious problem. He returned to the entrance to the medical shelter and rallied his men. Morale was low, and something had to be done urgently.

'All right, listen. The Retrograde element is out in strength. They operate as individual groups, not a combined tactical force, but they're dangerous for all that. More dangerous, perhaps. Emergency discipline procedures obtain from this point on. Desertion, looting or insubordination will suffer the highest penalty.' There was a final order to add. Commonsense told Brazen that one man was behind this new development, and the culprit must be captured. 'The prime object is to find the Doctor. I want him brought to me alive.'

But Brazen had been chased completely out of the Doctor's thoughts by the real terror he could see now in Turlough's eyes. He looked up from the dazed face of the young man, and said sharply to Mr Range, 'Right, that settles it. No further, Mr Range. Stay here with Turlough. I'm going on alone.'

There was no arguing with the Doctor when he was in this mood, as Mr Range discovered. He settled down on the spot, unfolding a blanket from the bag he had been cautious enough to bring with him, and made Turlough as comfortable as possible while the Doctor went off to investigate.

He heard the Doctor's name being called, and looked up to see Tegan running down the corridor towards them. 'So here you all are,' she said cheerfully. And then she noticed Turlough's face. 'What's up with him?'

Quickly Mr Range told her what had happened. He explained that the Doctor had gone to investigate, leaving strict instructions that no one was to go with him. 'He went this way?' was all she said.

'Wait!' said Mr Range. 'You can't . . .' But Tegan seemed not to hear. She set off down the tunnel saying, 'Must see the Doctor. I'll be back in a jiff.'

'So they're Tractators!' exclaimed the Doctor under his breath. At the point where he stood, the tunnel opened out into a large cave. In the middle of it, rigid with fear, Norna stood surrounded by a ring of silver creatures, each larger than a man. Their insect-like bodies were scaled like fish, and from their underbellies a pale luminescence emanated. They seemed to be exerting some sort of force on the girl, holding her immobile in the centre of their circle of concentration.

The Doctor heard a sudden intake of breath, and turned to see Tegan standing beside him. 'Get back, Tegan,' he hissed. 'These creatures are deadly.'

'I'm with you, Doc,' she whispered in a voice that was far from confident. She clung to the Doctor's hand, and he heard her gasp, 'No! What are they doing now?' One of the silver creatures in the ring, larger than the others and apparently the leader, had risen up on his innumerable rear legs and was swaying his body to and fro, directing his glowing underbelly towards Norna.

The Doctor could feel the presence of powerful invisible forces, as one by one the other creatures followed suit, lifting their bodies to join in the motion. He pushed Tegan behind him, watching the sickly swaying of that hideous luminous circle around Norna swell into a tidal wave of white underbellies that sucked at her, threatening to drag her flesh from her bones.

7

The Force Takes Hold

Brazen and his Orderlies methodically took up their positions in front of the colony-ship. They all understood that killing was to be avoided as far as possible. Brazen was concerned to demonstrate clearly to the Rets – and to his own men for that matter – that order was now restored. 'Don't hurry into it. Let them see who's controlling the situation.'

At the sight of them the few Retrograde looters in the region of the colony-ship entrance began to back away. Some dropped the food and supplies they had managed to gather and scuttled off in all directions; others took the opportunity of darting out from cover to collect what fell, and there were some savage scuffles for possession.

But as Brazen's men advanced across the open space the last of the Retrogrades vanished. When they reached the ramp that led up to the entrance, Brazen signalled to his Orderlies to be cautious. At the door they halted, and heard an ominous whispering emanating from inside the ship.

Brazen made a sign to the others to stay back, and pushed the door open with his club. There was no one in sight, but the moment he stepped in through the doorway the whispering seemed louder, as if the thousand dead souls who had flown the flight from Earth had regained their tongues to speak of their terrible history.

And then in the miasma of sounds that might have been

the wind in the corridors, Brazen focused on a noise that was specific and real; the creak of the door folding back against the wall. Someone was hiding behind it.

Brazen threw his weight against the door. The heavy metal plating slammed back against the wall, and a stifled cry came from behind it. Brazen raised his club, and let the door swing back from the wall. The looter clutching a crushed box of food in his arms was . . . Cockerill!

Brazen held his club threateningly against the man's throat. 'This is desertion, Cockerill. Anything to say about it?'

Cockerill stared back in defiance. 'Let go of me. It's all over now.'

'For you, yes,' snapped Brazen. Cockerill seemed unimpressed by these threats, even though the Orderlies were now surrounding him. 'For Frontios,' he said in a voice loud enough for them all to hear. 'The leadership's destroyed. Haven't you heard? Plantagenet has been eaten by the earth.'

Brazen's eyes narrowed. 'Where did you glean this intelligence?'

'Common knowledge,' shrugged Cockerill.

'Knowledge, Cockerill? You're talking like a Retrograde.'

A smile twisted Cockerill's lips, although the pressure of the cudgel on his throat was nearly choking him. 'We're all Rets now, Brazen.'

The whisper of Cockerill's last phrase seemed to echo back from the depth of the propulsion chamber. Brazen lowered the cudgel and took the crushed box of loot. While he cursorily inspected it, rooting through the collection of bread cubes, sugar tablets and preserved meat packs, Cockerill's insolent voice continued. 'The planet's doomed, Brazen. You all know it – except the ones who are too stupid to think for themselves.'

Brazen handed the box back to Cockerill. 'Enough food to last a few days . . . What then?'

Cockerill shrugged. The Orderlies had taken him by the arms, but now Brazen made a sign to them to release him. 'It's not easy living inside the system, Cockerill. But living outside it takes more than you've got.' They were walking to the door. 'You're letting me go?' Cockerill's world-weary tone did not conceal the note of surprise.

Brazen stepped aside to let him go out. 'I don't want you,' he said. Still clutching the crushed box Cockerill smiled insolently, expecting a trick. When he was halfway down the ramp he turned again to look at Brazen, but the granite face of the Chief Orderly told him nothing of his motives or his intentions.

Cockerill ran, heading for the sand dunes beyond the settlement. Brazen raised a hand to shade the light from his eyes, watching the departure of the Orderly turned Retrograde. The swiftly moving figure reached the low buildings on the other side of the open space when Brazen saw, as he expected, a group of lurking Rets fall on him and savage him, making off with the little box and its pathetic collection of food.

Cockerill lay on the ground in a crumpled heap. One of the Orderlies suggested going to get him, but Brazen shook his head. 'Leave him. He's made his choice.' Brazen knew himself to be a man of no great eloquence or invention – no Captain Revere. But he had an understanding of the world.

He set guards on the door, and initiated the search of the colony ship.

Watching the hypnotic ebb and flow of the swaying creatures around Norna, the Doctor found it hard to think. The first thing that came to mind was to break their deadly concentration by creating a diversion. 'Plan A', as he mentally labelled it, had the considerable disadvantage of endangering himself and Tegan without any guarantee of saving Norna. The second thing that came to mind was that there was no time to devise 'Plan B'. So without even a preliminary warning to Tegan he began waving his phosphor lamp and shouting.

The creatures that Turlough had called Tractators took no notice. Norna's arms and legs were by now splayed out like the spokes of a wheel and her hair stood up on her head in spikes. Tegan joined in the Doctor's waving and shouting with a frenzy of enthusiasm that threatened to send her lamp crashing against the rock wall. The Doctor snatched it from her for safety, and then realised that safety was not what the situation required. With all his force he smashed it against the side of the tunnel and hurled it into the cave.

There was a flash and a hissing sound. Seething luminous foam spilled across the ground, and for the first time the Tractators interrupted their deadly rhythm and turned away from Norna.

The break in their concentration had an extraordinary effect. Norna began to rise into the air, travelling in an arc that to the Doctor's eye looked suspiciously like an object falling through a distorted gravity field. As consternation grew among the silvery creatures, sending them scurrying across the cave, Norna came tumbling to the ground almost at Tegan's feet.

'Run!' the Doctor shouted to the two girls. 'Get out of here.' But he showed no sign of escaping himself, and Tegan said indignantly, 'Not likely, Doctor. Not without you.'

The Doctor was in no mood to argue. He thrust his lamp on Tegan. 'Out, I said. Quickly!'

The moment they were gone the Doctor paused to look around for a weapon, but all he could find was a large rock. The last flickers of flame were licking up from the luminous green pool, and in that doubtful light he fancied he glimpsed the creatures rallying in a small side tunnel. With the vague idea of obstructing their return to the cave he picked up the rock and carried it towards them. But when he got a better view of the tunnel the creatures had gone.

Or so it seemed for a moment. But as he turned he found one of the Tractators directly behind him. The two bulbous eyes on either side of the shrimp-like head widened like glossy black mouths, and in the shock of the confrontation the Doctor dropped the rock on his foot. He opened his mouth to cry out in pain, and then realised that the rock had not fallen. He looked down to find it hovering a few inches above the ground.

There was an element of the ludicrous about that moment before the rock was suddenly whisked away, to fall somewhere on the far side of the cave. But the Doctor was not amused. It was not his own immediate physical danger that chilled his blood, but a quite sudden, horrifying confirmation of the partially formulated thoughts he had been accumulating ever since the inexplicable destruction of the TARDIS. Now there was no doubt. The Tractators were in command of gravitational forces of immense power.

Mr Range was examining Turlough, holding his phosphor lamp up to the young man's glazed face, when Tegan arrived with Norna. He folded his daughter in his arms and made her comfortable on the ground beside Turlough. 'And the Doctor?' he asked.

'Give me a lamp,' said Tegan tersely. 'I'm going back for him.' Mr Range stopped her. 'You can't. It's dangerous!'

But Norna clutched at her father's arm. 'We can't leave him there. He saved my life.'

The cautious scientist thought for a moment, then began rummaging about in the bag he had brought with him, to produce three more of the phosphor lamps. He handed one to Norna. 'You stay here with Turlough. Don't move from this spot.'

But Tegan firmly rejected Mr Range's offer to come with her. 'The Doctor's my responsibility. Turlough and Norna need you here.' And with that she ran off down the tunnel.

Mr Range watched the green glow of her lamp recede into the darkness and shook his head. 'It's so foolish to go down the tunnels alone. These creatures . . .' Coming to a painful decision, he picked up one of the phosphor lamps and turned to Norna. 'Look after the boy. I won't be long.' And he set off down the tunnel following Tegan.

Step by step the Doctor backed away from the Tractator, trying not to show his fear. He had no doubt about its malevolent tendencies, but this one seemed still a little confused after the explosion of the phosphor lamp, now a dying luminescent pool on the floor of the cave. The Doctor wished he had another lamp, or an armful of them. As it was, the only asset to hand was the large boulder he was making for. It was far too big to lift, but might provide temporary cover while he thought up his next move.

He ducked behind it, hoping the dazed Tractator would lose interest. But the creature continued advancing with a sinister shuffling sound. When the sound stopped, the Doctor found the silence even more unnerving and peered round the boulder to see what was happening.

The creature had reared up on its hind legs, and the faint white glow from its underbelly was growing stronger. The boulder the Doctor was hiding behind began to shift forward, pulled by some immense invisible power. Slowly it gathered momentum, rolling towards the Tractator.

In trying to remain concealed the Doctor had no choice but to follow, keeping it between him and the Tractator. The creature was backing away now towards the small side tunnel, dragging the boulder behind him. The plan was obviously to clear the boulder out of the cave and leave the Doctor with no cover. But the Doctor had a plan of his own.

'Come on, my little beauty . . .' he muttered to the boulder. The Tractator had almost reached the small side tunnel when suddenly the Doctor put his hands under the boulder and with a mighty heave helped it on its way. As he had hoped, the additional acceleration wrong-footed the Tractator, and it skittered backwards into the tunnel.

That was its mistake. The boulder hit the tunnel with a thud that shook rocks loose from the roof, and jammed into position, trapping the Tractator behind it. 'A bold stroke,' said the Doctor, straightening up. 'A well-bowled boulder.' Pleased with his efforts, but only too aware of the temporary nature of the solution, the Doctor backed against the wall, not wanting to make a move until he knew where the other Tractators were.

Faintly he heard Tegan calling his name, and saw the faint light advancing down the tunnel. 'Tegan!' he called back. 'Stay where you are – I'm coming.' And he began running towards her.

Or rather, tried to. But although his legs were pumping hard, he made very little progress. It was as if the air in the tunnel had turned to treacle, and the rock floor under his feet were a sort of conveyor belt running backwards. The mysterious force that the Tractators controlled was dragging him back towards the big cave.

He tried to fight it, putting all his strength into the run. But the force was increasing, and soon he was merely running on the spot. Out of breath he called to Tegan, 'No good . . . can't make it. . . . Get back!' Invisible strings snatched at his feet and he fell flat on his face.

Out of the darkness he saw Tegan running towards him. 'Doctor! Hang on, I'll give you a hand.'

'No!' he shouted. 'Stay clear.' He tried to scramble to his feet, but the same unseen influence dragged him back along the tunnel away from her. Ignoring his warning, Tegan grabbed his hands, trying to pull him forward. 'I've got you, Doctor. It's OK. . . .' He managed to stand, but now the two of them were being pulled backwards together down the tunnel, Tegan clinging tightly to his cricket coat.

'Some sort of gravity beam . . .' panted the Doctor.

'From the Tractators.' And then a new light appeared, and the Doctor glimpsed the rapidly receding figure of Mr Range, waving his lamp and shouting to him. The Doctor called back to him, 'Stay away! Get everyone back to the research room immediately. It's too dangerous . . .'

And then Mr Range and his lamp vanished, and the Doctor and Tegan were whisked round a bend in the tunnel. Faster and faster the gravity beam drew them on. 'Doctor!' Tegan shouted. 'Think of something.'

'I am,' said the Doctor. 'Lots of things.' But, he might have added, nothing that quite fitted the gravity of the occasion. Except that he was in no mood for jokes.

Norna shivered. Her body still ached from top to toe, but the pain was gone now, and she was able to attend to Turlough, who still appeared to be in a state of shock. She wished her father would come back, or better still that the Doctor was with them.

Turlough began to talk again, and she leant closer to hear what he was saying. 'My home . . . Tractators. Seen all this . . . Know it before . . .' There was much more of the same, wild rambling words that made little sense. And then her father came stumbling back along the tunnel.

'Quick, we must go to the surface and get help.'

'But the Doctor?'

'His strict orders,' said Mr Range. They began to lift Turlough, and the words started spilling out again. 'They were there, waiting . . .' came the distant voice, '. . . destroying us from inside.' It seemed to be coming up from his past, and his glazed eyes were fastened on some invisible memory picture that sent shivers through him. 'Tractators . . . Once, long ago . . . on my planet.'

'You remember them?' Norna prompted quietly. Her father was trying to hurry them all along the tunnel, but Norna persuaded him to pause a little. What Turlough had to say could easily be important.

'We remember them,' said the young man. 'All of us . . . the people of my planet . . . will never forget . . .'

Mr Range bent over Turlough. 'This sounds like deep ancestral memory.' It was as if he were remembering the history of his people, events that had happened to members of his race who were long dead. 'Go back in your mind, Turlough. Far, far back . . .'

Turlough's eyes closed. 'Tractators – once, long ago, our home was . . .' Now in a deep trance he shuddered at the memory he was unlocking, and his voice came as a strained whisper. 'An infection . . .' he said. 'An infection of the planet.'

Tegan had begun to think that the force dragging her and the Doctor ever deeper into the Tractators' tunnel system would never let go. But as the rock walls flashed past with increasing speed she began to realise that the discomfort of this method of travel was nothing to what would happen once they reached wherever it was the Tractators were taking them. Up to now at least she had the comfort of the Doctor's reassuring hand in hers. But the acceleration was gradually pulling them apart, and at last she had to let go. 'Lamp . . .' he shouted over his shoulder. 'Give it to me . . .'

She threw it, unprepared for the effect of the distorted gravitation that twisted it through the air in a strange, swift arc. In stretching out to catch it the Doctor barely avoided losing his balance again. 'What are you going to do?' she called.

The voice of the Doctor came back to her faintly over the rush of wind in her ears. 'Wait till we're close enough . . .'

The tunnel walls were almost a blur now, but at the end of the long straight section they were travelling along, she could just make out a junction where a smaller tunnel led off to one side. 'Ready?' shouted the Doctor.

'When you are, Doc! But to do what?'

'Grab the wall! Now!' And he threw himself at the point where the smaller tunnel split off. She hurtled into him, grabbed at his coat and then his hair, and eventually managed to secure a perilous handhold on the rock corner. Now the Doctor was clinging to her, his legs flailing like flags in a high wind. 'I've got you, Doc,' she bellowed. 'Don't know how long I can hold on . . .' Already she felt her fingers slipping on the smooth rock surface.

'Hold my coat,' he shouted back. He released his hand from her and began fumbling with the phosphor lamp. Tegan changed her grip and held him by the back of the collar and the coat-tail. With both hands free the Doctor was able to grip the lamp. With a savage twist he snapped it in two and hurled the halves as far forwards as he could along the tunnel.

There was a green flash as the lamp hit the ground. To Tegan's horror the Doctor began slowly slipping forwards out of his coat and into the sudden wall of flame that leapt up in front of them. 'Doctor! Come back!'

And then quite suddenly the wind stopped, and the terrible force that had been tearing at them was turned off, as if a switch had been thrown. The silence caught the Doctor half in and half out of his coat. He shrugged it on again and, dusting himself down, walked back along the tunnel to where Tegan stood panting for breath.

'Nice work, Tegan. We'd better get out of here.' Taking his outstretched hand, and silently swearing never to let go of it until they were above ground again, Tegan ran with the Doctor into the small side tunnel.

8

Eaten by the Earth

The journey out of the tunnel was slow for Norna and her father. Turlough, supported between them, was taking the weight on his feet now, but he was still not properly conscious, and they had to keep stopping for a rest.

'Steady, young man,' said Mr Range as Turlough's feet stumbled on a loose stone. 'Not much further to go.' He was anxious to hurry on, but Norna called out, 'Father, wait a minute.' She signalled to him to bring the lamp over to where she was inspecting the base of one of the walls.

'We've no time to waste . . .' he began irritably, and then broke off when he saw what she had found. Low down on the cave wall was a roughly hewn plaque. As he stooped down, the lamp light fell on the inscription, crudely carved in the rock with some metal instrument.

'LEVEL TWO. NO MINERALS OF VALUE DETECTED AS FAR AS THIS POINT. THIS DAY OF FRONTIOS ALPHA 14404, CAPTAIN REVERE'

'That proves it!' Norna exclaimed. 'Captain Revere must have known about these caves and tunnels.' Her father nodded. 'And more than that, perhaps.'

'You think he knew about the creatures?' Norna asked, tracing with her fingers the name carved at the bottom of the plaque. 'But why not tell the people of Frontios?'

'The conspiracy of silence!' exclaimed her father. 'I've been collecting evidence all these years . . .' He unhooked his glasses and rubbed the bridge of his nose. Now was the time to tell his daughter what he had heard from Tegan about the dreadful disappearance of Plantagenet in the medical shelter. It seemed clear now that there was a connection between the unaccountable deaths he had been recording and the creatures that Turlough called Tractators.

At the mention of the creatures a shuddering sigh came from Turlough's lips. They turned to see their young friend staring into the blurred rippled reflections in the walls, as if mesmerised by what he saw there. 'The earth is hungry . . . It waits to eat . . .'

'Look!' exclaimed Norna, 'Turlough's forcing himself to remember . . .'

Mr Range pushed his glasses back on his nose and picked up his bag. 'We must hurry. 'We must get help.' But Norna stayed kneeling on the ground beside Turlough. 'This may be the help we need, father. It's here that he remembers.' She put her hand on the young man's shoulder and looked with him into the black distorting mirror of the walls. 'You can see them, under the ground of your own planet? What are they doing?'

Turlough's lips moved. 'Growing. Multiplying. Spreading the infection.'

'How do they do that?'

He shook his head. 'I can't see it. There's a wall.' Norna recognised it as an emotional block, something that Turlough found himself unable to face. 'Try to get through the wall.' Her voice was soothing. He felt her cool hand slip into his, and heard her telling him the black, smooth walls were really glass, and quite easy to see into.

At first the shiny surface showed only the distorted image of his own pale face, a freckled smudge and two wide blue eyes that stared back at him. But as he watched, the flesh seemed to decay. He saw the gleam of white bone and the cavernous sockets of a skull. He cried out and shut his eyes, cringing away from the vision. 'Evil! I can't . . . speak . . .'

'That's enough,' said Mr Range, pulling Turlough to his feet. 'We must get him out of here.' His temperature was dropping, and Mr Range knew he needed to be somewhere warm. Fortunately there was only a little further to go before they recognised the excavation area under the research room and the rectangular trap door that led back to safety.

Or so they thought. But no sooner had Mr Range set his foot on the ladder than a voice came booming out from above them. 'Mr Range . . . We've been waiting for you.'

Mr Range and Norna looked up to see Brazen and his Orderlies surrounding the rim of the trap door. The Chief Orderly waved a folder. 'I have a most interesting file here, Mr. Range. Its contents amount to a charge of sedition.'

The tunnel in which the Doctor and Tegan now found themselves was lit by an eerie glow from a naturally formed window. Signalling to Tegan to keep well down, the Doctor lifted his head and peered over the edge of the low rock wall. He was not prepared for what he saw next. He was looking down on an enormous cavern, bathed in light from some source he couldn't identify. Tractators were milling everywhere, engaged in a busy pattern of activity that reminded him of ants: exerting their force to move rocks and strange fabrications of metal and wood.

He found Tegan beside him. 'They're building something,' she whispered. The Doctor nodded. 'A nest, perhaps.' Tegan shuddered, and the Doctor reminded her that it takes all sorts to make a universe. As they resumed their exploration of the tunnel Tegan accused him of making excuses for the creatures and the terrible use they made of their gravitational power.

She thought the Doctor was taking broadmindedness too far when he suggested that they suspend judgement until they knew more about the Tractators, but this was no place to have an argument. 'Turlough's the one to tell us that, if only he can unlock his mind,' he said.

'We have to get back first,' Tegan pointed out, and the Doctor startled her by hissing, 'Get back!' She turned to him indignantly. 'What's wrong with getting back?'

'Against the wall!' The Doctor grabbed her and pulled her to one side. She looked in the direction of his gaze and saw a Tractator in the tunnel ahead of them. Its luminous underbelly was curved in a great convex arch, facing up towards the roof of the tunnel.

Tegan pressed herself flat against the wall. 'There's something up there it's trying to get down,' said the Doctor slowly. 'I'm going to try an experiment.' He fished in his pocket and produced – of all things – a cricket ball.

For several hours Cockerill had been lying face down on the ground at the edge of the settlement where the sand dunes began. Consciousness came and went, enough for him to be aware of the congealing blood that flowed from the cut across his head, and a dizzying pain every time he tried to stir.

His mind cleared again suddenly on feeling a sharp tugging at his right hand. He opened his eyes and tried to focus on it, but he could only trace the arm as far as the elbow. From there on it was buried in the grey soil.

He tried to lift it, but his efforts were answered by another tug, pulling it deeper. Despite the pain he managed to raise his head. The earth around him had taken on a sponge-like texture, and it crumbled under him when he tried to lift himself to his feet. He felt himself sinking, further and further into it.

A small group of Retrogrades had drifted together from their hiding places in the sand dunes, and stood at a safe distance watching him. He called out to them, but none of them moved.

Whether from fear, or long exposure to suffering, they offered no expression of sympathy. Struggling face down, Cockerill sank into the unrelenting earth, as certain as the impassive onlookers that there was no one to save him.

He was wrong about that. Not that the Doctor, at that moment weighing the cricket ball in his hand, knew anything about Cockerill and his plight. 'Can't we just . . . leave the Tractator alone?' asked Tegan under her breath.

'A good opportunity to measure the gravitational force-field,' said the Doctor, and he lobbed the cricket ball carefully in the direction of the creature.

The ball looped in the air, travelling in an extraordinary curve around the Tractator before bounding against the wall and returning the way it came. The Doctor caught it deftly. 'No time for games, Doctor,' whispered Tegan.

The Doctor's face was grim. 'This is something a little more scientific. I want to see how directional this force of theirs is. Just one more . . .'

'Too late, Doc. It's seen us.'

The Doctor had already let go of the ball. The Tractator glanced down towards it, and it swerved in mid-flight and headed directly for the glowing underbelly. The Doctor grabbed Tegan's hand, and without waiting to see what happened next they turned and ran back down the tunnel in the direction they had come.

The group of Rets around Cockerill, growing in number as his struggles became more violent, had stood in silence up to now. But a whisper went round them all when he managed to extract the upper part of his body from the crumbling ground and gesticulate to them with wild, flailing arms. When he freed his legs they gasped. But the group, swelled by now to a crowd, was reduced once more to silent astonishment when they saw him stand upright and walk towards them.

A whisper crackled around the crowd, like a fire in a dry bush. 'What is his name? How has he done this? He out-lived the hunger of the earth. A man who can do that can do anything.'

The questioning went on and on until Mr Range was wearied almost to the point of anger. Behind the table, dwarfed by the huge portrait of Captain Revere that dominated the State Room, sat his patient and unruffled questioner, Brazen's Deputy, her voice oozing a chill formality that for the moment forced Mr Range to keep his temper. At each reply to her questions she took careful notes, writing in an unhurried hand.

Beside the Deputy, out of deference to the missing leader, Plantagenet's chair was left empty. His second in command, Chief Orderly Brazen, was pacing restlessly back and forth past the two Orderlies guarding the door. Distancing himself from the proceedings, Brazen glanced only occasionally in the direction of Mr Range, but his eye fell more than once on the low bench to the side of the room, where Norna was tending to Turlough. In his mesmerised state the Doctor's young companion seemed unconscious of his surroundings, but now and again a low murmur rose from his lips.

'Do I understand then, Mr Range,' said the Deputy, looking up from her notes, 'that you admit to keeping private and secret medical records?'

'I am the Chief Science Officer,' replied Mr Range with dignity.

'Of course. And these records purport in part to record a history of "mysterious disappearances"?'

'The records are accurate,' Mr Range insisted. 'Since our first arrival on this planet there have been cases—'

'Yes, yes, Mr Range,' interrupted the Deputy in an unruffled voice. 'We all know the myths going about the place. No need to elaborate them here.'

Mr Range turned to Brazen and called across the State Room. 'But are they myths? That's the point!'

Brazen waved an impatient hand. 'Address the Deputy, please, Mr Range. It's the facts we're after, not a public debate.'

'These are facts! Bodies of the dead that have not been recovered . . . work personnel in the quarry unaccounted for. I even have one reliable eye witness account of a corpse disappearing into the earth.'

The words tumbled out of Mr Range's mouth. Brazen stopped pacing, but the Deputy took the outburst in her stride. 'Quite, Mr Range. But for some reason you chose to keep these miracles secret.'

Mr Range leaned forward across the table, his eyes angry behind the steel frames of his glasses. 'The State made them a secret. I merely collected the records.'

Brazen strode over to the table. 'I'm a plain-speaking man, Mr Range. You can't hedge with me. You've been collecting this garbage in an attempt to subvert law and order on Frontios. I'm right? Admit it.'

There was a moment of silence. 'Plantagenet accuses me of that?' asked Mr Range in a quieter voice.

The Deputy nodded. 'That is correct.'

Playing his trump card Mr Range jabbed a finger at the empty chair beside the Deputy. 'Then where is he?'

For the first time the Deputy allowed her mask of officialdom to slip. She glanced uneasily across to Brazen, who, however, made no response. 'I know why he isn't here!' continued Mr Range. 'The Doctor's friend told me what she saw in the hospital. Frontios "buries its own dead" – that's what they say, isn't it?'

The Deputy permitted herself a smile. 'So runs the myth.'

'She saw that myth,' said Mr Range. 'She saw Plantagenet being "eaten by the earth".'

The Deputy was shaken by this news, but was saved from

having to make a formal response by a cry from Turlough. Norna tried to quiet him, but the Deputy was already on her feet, demanding indignantly, 'He has some contribution to offer?'

Turlough's voice echoed across the State Room. ' "Eaten by the earth". They live in the ground below, pulling us to them in our times of weakness. Dead or alive, their forces tug at our bodies . . .'

The Deputy sat down again, dismissing the interruption. 'Please, we have work to do here . . .' But Brazen silenced her with an abrupt gesture and strode over to Turlough. 'What do you know about all this?'

'Leave him alone,' said Norna. 'He's in shock. He needs warmth and rest.'

'And I need answers,' said Brazen. He waved the Orderlies away. 'Wait outside. I'll accept no interruptions from anybody.' Then he added pointedly to the Deputy, 'Off the record, I think.' She rose and followed the two Orderlies out of the room.

'Now then, young man,' said Brazen when the room was cleared of officials. ' "They", you said. Who's "they"?'

Range came to Turlough's defence. 'I tell you, Brazen, he's in no state to be questioned.'

'You're out of order, Mr Range!' boomed the Chief Orderly. 'If there is a grain of truth in this story of yours, these are urgent matters of state. You expect me to delay the investigation because a young man is feeling delicate?' And with that he settled himself on the bench beside the Doctor's young companion, and said in a voice that was almost kindly, 'Name's Turlough, eh? All right, Turlough, I want to hear all about this . . .'

9

The Excavating Machine

At any moment during their escape from the Tractator, the Doctor expected to feel the invisible trawl-net of that gravitational force pulling them back into its clutches. He had run as he had never run before, dragging Tegan with him until their legs ached and their lungs were almost bursting. But it seemed, as they paused for breath at last, that they were free. Tegan recovered first, and wanted to talk of practical things, like finding the way out.

The Doctor was running his fingertips over the smooth surface of the wall. 'Sometimes it's easier to look for the way in and work backwards.'

Tegan tugged at his hand. 'Come on, Doctor, you won't find it there. All these walls look the same.'

'Ah, but they aren't,' replied the Doctor, stooping to pick up a handful of chippings from the floor. 'What does that tell you?'

'Just loose chippings,' said Tegan, unimpressed.

'Tegan, how many times have I got to remind you – nothing is "just" anything. Everything is a small clue to everything else. There's a nexus between objects.'

'Yes, all right, all right,' she said testily. She had heard his lecture on early Wittgenstein before, and now was not the time for a repeat. 'Doctor . . . the point?'

He weighed the chippings in his hand. 'These have been

machined – recently – from that wall. And in two stages.'
He took her to a section of tunnel they had already passed,
where the walls were noticeably rougher, carved to a flat
surface but not yet polished.

'They have machines . . .?' asked Tegan.

'That's what it looks like,' the Doctor replied. 'And
functionally sophisticated ones at that.' It was clear to him
now that the Tractators were creating an extensive and
elaborate tunnel system using pupose-built devices. Multi-
stage processes like these would involve planning, construction of equipment, resource management, and execu-
tion on a huge scale.

'Insect-like I grant you,' the Doctor went on, as they
made their way along the tunnel. 'But these are no ordinary
insects. They have highly-refined powers of abstract reason-
ing. And in case you hadn't noticed . . . they also seem to
have turned on the lights . . .'

Tegan thought it had been getting lighter around them. It
was the same sort of illumination they had seen when they
looked down on the cavern, a pale white glow diffusing
from the walls. 'Does that mean they're watching us?' she
asked uneasily.

A group of Tractators had gathered with their leader around
a cage suspended in the middle of the large cavern. The
words of Tegan and the Doctor, amplified by the peculiar
geography of the tunnel system, echoed down to them with
every syllable intact.

A human form stirred in the cage. The leader of the
Tractators turned its head to a tall narrow trolley that
floated a foot or so above the ground, and drew the small
construction towards him with the tiniest shake of his head.
Mounted on it was the head and one arm of a dead Colonist,
connected by improvised metalwork to a swinging pendulum.

The hideous device spoke, translating the thoughts of the
Tractator leader for the benefit of the prisoner in the cage. 'I

am the translator that speaks for the Gravis, first among the Tractators. There is a man called "the Doctor" who wanders in our tunnel system. What do you know of him?'

A hand stretched weakly out from the cage, causing the translator to edge back out of reach. 'You have nothing to say?' it croaked, its dead mouth moving to the click of the pendulum. 'Then it is time, I think, we fetched this Doctor to us.' The Tractators gathered around the Gravis shuffled their bodies in agreement. 'We will send – the machine.'

In the State Room Brazen pressed on with his questions about the Tractators. 'Organised, intelligent . . . Not much of an enemy profile. I want to know what they're about, and why.'

Mr Range intervened. 'Please. That's enough. Deep ancestral memory pictures can be dangerous when they break through the conscious mind like this. Leave the boy alone. If anyone is on trial here it's me.'

'Not a trial, Mr Range – a pooling of information. Something we should have done decades ago.' Brazen lifted his big bulk from the bench, terminating the interrogation of Turlough.

'You had the chance,' said Mr Range.

'No – because you had the evidence, locked in a drawer. If you had showed us that . . . the dear good Captain who with his bare hands held together this shambles we call Frontios . . . Captain Revere could well be alive today.'

Norna spoke up for her father. 'Captain Revere knew about these creatures. He must have done!' She told Brazen about the plaque inscribed with his name. 'It's Captain Revere's fault! Why didn't he tell us?'

'And add to the rumours and unrest?' said Brazen. 'How little you know about leadership. You can't broadcast socially sensitive information until you're in control of the facts.'

'But if we'd known for sure . . .' Norna began.

'We could have done what?' Brazen paused for an answer, but Norna could find nothing to say, so he went on, 'These "Tractators" the boy describes . . . They explain to my satisfaction the unspeakable events we've witnessed.'

'Not witnessed,' Mr Range interrupted. 'If we're being particular about this, you and I have not actually seen—'

Brazen raised a hand to silence him. 'I have, Mr Range,' he said slowly. 'Come with me . . . I want to show you something.'

The Doctor stuck his finger in his mouth and held it up in the air. 'You're never without a sense of direction while there's an air flow. Air flows from A to B. You usually want to be at B. Or at A.'

'I don't want to be at A or B, thanks all the same,' said Tegan, by now very anxious to be out of the tunnels altogether. 'I want to be back in the . . .' She nearly said 'TARDIS'. The Doctor cleared his throat; she had touched on a painful subject. 'Mmm . . . Well, we can forget about the TARDIS. It's probably scattered in bits across the whole of Frontios.'

In the silence that followed this remark Tegan thought she could hear distant activity. She put her ear to the wall. Something like the sound of fingernails scraping on glass echoed down the tunnel from a long way away.

'Natural rock settlement,' said the Doctor, fishing out a pencil and a scrap of paper from one of his many pockets. 'Now quiet, I need to do some air-flow calculations . . .'

Tegan put her ear against the wall again, but the sound seemed to have stopped. She waited while the Doctor fiddled with his figures, but the suspense quickly became too much for her. 'For pity's sake, Doc. I don't see how mathematics is going to get us out of this.'

'How do you think the pilot steers his ship, the millionaire manages his millions, the Time Lord controls his destiny?'

Tegan snorted with impatience. 'And a fine controller of your destiny you turned out to be!'

'I may not be Rassilon,' said the Doctor, waving the paper. 'But I do know the way out of here . . .' He broke off suddenly, catching hold of her arm. 'Wait! That's it, isn't it!' The sound Tegan had heard was now clearly audible, a strange scraping and thudding echoing down the tunnel.

Tegan was frightened now. 'What is it?' The Doctor trickled a handful of the loose chippings through his fingers. 'The machine that did this. And it seems to be coming this way.'

Brazen's swift march out of the State Room had taken them back to the research room, to the very edge of the excavation area. In the light of Brazen's phosphor lamp Norna and her father could see clearly the indented shape in the mottled rock. Norna gasped. It was the outline of a man. 'Captain Revere,' said Brazen.

'But the State funeral . . .' said Mr Range. 'We all saw the body.'

'The face was burnt,' Norna remembered. 'Unrecognisable.' Brazen confirmed her thought with a nod.

'There had to be a corpse of some sort to keep public order.' He told them how he had seen Captain Brazen sucked into the earth in front of his eyes. 'He was badly injured by the falling timber-props, but he would have lived . . .'

'He may still be alive,' said a faraway voice. They had forgotten about Turlough, who had at last approached the dark rectangle in the floor, daring to look down into the earth he dreaded.

'Alive?' demanded Brazen. 'What do you mean?'

Mr Range took the young man by the shoulders. But Turlough would not be moved away from the excavation area, and was determined to speak. 'Captain Revere, and

Plantagenet too. The Tractators need living flesh. They need minds . . . as well as bodies.'

The translating machine rose in the air and hovered close to the cage. Driven through levers and articulating linkages by the steady beat of the pendulum, the dead arm reached out and shook the bars of the cage.

The prisoner spoke for the first time. 'What do you want with me? Who are you?'

The mouth on the hideous device hovering outside the bars began to move again in time to the ticking pendulum. Speaking the words of the Gravis, it said, 'The work of excavation is our task. Beneath the soil we can expand and populate the whole of Frontios. You understand? It is important that you understand. Speak. My translating device will hear you adequately.'

The prisoner behind the bars turned from the hideous talking machine to look the Gravis in the eye. Beneath the shock of white hair the deep scars of his face showed up against the pale skin. Thin and haggard and drained of strength, Plantagenet was barely recognisable. 'We will defeat your goal.'

'You do not know our goal,' came the answer from the translator. 'I have described our means. Once we have full control of Frontios, our plans are only just beginning.'

'You are evil,' declared Plantagenet, finding a vestige of strength in his anger. 'We will fight you to the last.'

'This is not a war, Plantagenet. It is a co-operation. You will see.'

Plantagenet gripped the bars of the cage. 'The colonists of Frontios will never co-operate with you.'

'But they do,' croaked the machine. 'We Tractators have devised an economical technology of excavation. But it needs a captive human mind to drive it.'

'Captive?' hissed Plantagenet. 'You keep slaves?'

'You will see, you will see,' clicked the horrible machine.

'Our old driver is nearing the end of his useful powers. But now we have another to take his place. Do we not, Plantagenet?'

Plantagenet drew back in horror as the meaning of the rhetorical question sank in.

In the research room, phosphor lamps were arrayed in a row along the edge of the descent to the excavation area. Heavy duty boots tramping down the corridor and across the research room floor, the members of the volunteer expeditionary force filed in for duty. They handed their shotguns to an Orderly, who stacked them up in a line against the wall, and in exchange each received a short club. Brazen judged that the shotguns, unreliable at the best of times, would be downright dangerous underground.

Brazen had positioned himself at the edge of the excavation area, looking over the volunteers as they descended, and handing each of them a phosphor lamp from the row. 'Good man, Kernighan . . . Brace up there, Ritchie, you're a volunteer. And remember we're all going to be privileged to sit down and eat with Plantagenet on our return. . . .'

Norna was laying out food rations on a trestle table set up for the occasion. At the one end of the table sat Turlough with his head in his hands. 'You didn't let anybody down,' Norna said to reassure him. He had recovered completely from his trance-like state, and had been talking to her quite normally until Brazen had announced the expedition.

'Who cares?' he said. 'This isn't my kind of thing, anyway. Caves and tunnels, mooching about under-ground . . . !' It was Mr Range who had insisted that Turlough was in no fit state to return to the tunnels.

On the other side of the room Brazen was in whispered consultation with him now about just that subject. 'Not Turlough, Chief Orderly,' Mr Range said firmly.

But Brazen was not easily persuaded. 'We need someone who knows the terrain.'

Mr Range was insistent. 'He'll be a liability to your expedition. I'll come with you and show you the way.'

'I'd prefer you to stay here with your daughter,' said Brazen. 'The Rets are on the rampage outside, and it could get nasty above ground too.' Norna had overheard this last remark of Brazen's and came over to join them. 'I don't need looking after. Anyway, Turlough's here.'

Brazen shrugged. 'All right, Mr Range. I'll take your offer.' The two of them collected their lamps and followed the Orderlies down into the excavation area.

At the edge of the descent one lamp remained. While Norna continued laying out the food around him, Turlough eyed it from across the room. Every time she glanced across at him she noticed him staring it out, as if the solitary lamp presented a silent challenge.

'Don't torture yourself,' she said eventually. 'Nobody expects you to go back there.'

'Of course they don't. I'm Turlough.' As if on an impulse he got up from the table and came over to her, holding out his hands as fists, inviting her to choose. 'What's this for?' she asked.

'Decision time,' Turlough replied enigmatically. Norna laughed and touched his left fist. He opened his hand. There was a small silver coin in it. 'That's it, then,' he said. 'I'm going.'

'No, don't be silly . . .' Norna ran to him, but had to stop to catch the coin he tossed over to her. 'You can't argue with fate,' he said. Norna looked at the coin: it had a hole in the centre. 'It's a two corpira piece,' said Turlough. 'You blow through the hole for luck.'

He seemed determined to go. Norna disdained anything so childishly superstitious as blowing through a coin, but she held out her empty hand to shake his. 'Good luck, then.' He shook her hand rather formally, collected the phosphor lamp, and then clambered down into the excavation area.

In the hand he had shaken she found a second two corpira piece. 'What a minute . . . !' But he had gone. Norna weighed the two coins in either hand, amused at his way of doing things. She did not notice the hatch in the roof inching open, and the hungry eyes of the Rets who gazed down through the gap at the table of food.

Down in the tunnel the Doctor and Tegan heard the whirring and scraping of the approaching excavating machine and ran on, stumbling in their haste. Suddenly the Doctor stopped and pulled Tegan back into a shallow niche in the tunnel wall. 'This is ridiculous,' said Tegan. 'Running round like rabbits in a hole in the ground. If you ask me—'

'Nobody is, Tegan. Now shush.'

'Guess I'm nervous,' Tegan went on. 'I get sort of chatty when I'm nervous. My mother was the same. Once we were in a fairground in Brisbane . . .'

'Stop it!' The Doctor wasn't in the mood for any of this. He picked up a pebble and tossed it in front of him. It curved sharply away and flew down the tunnel. 'I thought so!' he said in a whisper. 'Tractators, dead ahead. And more than one of them.' Tegan glanced over her shoulder. Behind them, somewhere beyond the bend of the tunnel she could hear the excavating machine coming ever nearer.

'We were crammed into one of those Big Dipper things with a lot of horrible people with ice creams,' whispered Tegan, 'and my mother turned round and said . . .'

'Excavating machine or the Tractators?' said the Doctor crisply. 'Take your pick.'

The ominous thudding and scraping was almost deafening now. Tegan could make out a huge shadowy shape filling the whole tunnel as it turned the corner. Whatever it was advancing on them, she preferred the Tractators. The Doctor evidently had the same thought; she took his hand and they made a dash together in the direction of the creatures they had come to loathe.

The tunnel debouched suddenly into the central cavern they had glimpsed through the natural window. Tegan gasped. Tractators were everywhere, and directly ahead stood a line of them, forming a most unwelcome welcoming committee.

'Too many,' shouted the Doctor. 'Back into the tunnel – quick.' But as they tried to run back the way they had come, their limbs became as heavy as lead. Escape was useless. The gravitational power of the Tractators had them hopelessly caught in its web.

In front of them the scraping, thudding sound of the excavator echoed louder and louder in the tunnel. They stared in horror at the machine that emerged into the light.

It was a repellent sight: a huge and hideous assembly of parts of human bodies, shaped something in the form of a giant Tractator. White bones tipped with metal cutters scraped against the rock, while rotting hands polished the surface smooth. Through illuminated windows in the body Tegan glimpsed more mechanically gesticulating human arms and legs in an advanced state of decay. It was a machine built from the dead.

But not just the dead. In a hollowed out area at the front of the machine, between the forward cutters that spun to left and to right, crouched a shape that was recognisably human. Tendrils of many colours connected the head into the machine, and as it emerged into the light they saw the figure was alive, a living mind enslaved to drive the machine.

Living, but in a fearfully wasted state. Tegan recognised the face from the portraits she had seen in the medical shelter and the State Room. It was Captain Revere.

10

Prisoners of the Gravis

The hideous excavating machine whirred to a halt in the mouth of the tunnel, blocking any escape by that route. But escape was impossible in any case, for the Doctor and Tegan were bound fast by the invisible force of the wall of Tractators in front of them.

The Doctor had already recognised one of the creatures as the leader by its greater size, and by the way the others seemed to defer to it. It glided forward now, carrying before it in its force-field the gruesome relic of humanity that had become its translating machine. As the pendulum clicked back and forth a thin, grating voice pulsed from the articulating mouth. 'Two specimens have come down to us from the world above in an undamaged state. This is a rare pleasure.'

Tegan's blood ran cold, but her fear was overwhelmed by a rush of talkativeness. 'I suppose you know you're dealing with a Time Lord,' she blurted out angrily.

The machine spoke again. 'Oh, we know the Doctor. At least by reputation.'

Tegan felt a restraining hand on her arm, and the Doctor was by her side, saying, 'Then perhaps you won't mind telling us who you are.'

Through the machine the Gravis introduced himself. 'We are the Tractators. At last after millenia as outcasts of the universe we have found a home. But of course you Time Lords must know that by now. Why else would the rulers of Gallifrey have sent you on this fruitless mission to interfere?'

Tegan took a deep breath, about to tell them they were completely wrong, but the Doctor's fingers tightened on her arm in warning. The ring of Tractators parted to let the Gravis move between them, and the Doctor and Tegan felt themselves being impelled in front of him. Across the cave the invisible force carried them, and into a low, wide tunnel that sloped upwards, narrowing as it went. Off to one side was a cave smaller than the others they had seen, and here they found themselves enclosed by walls that were chased with elaborate carvings.

'Our centre of operations,' said the Gravis. 'You see, Doctor, I do not fear you will take this information back to Gallifrey. You will never leave Frontios now.'

'You could be right, Gravis,' said the Doctor. 'For a small planet, Frontios is certainly very . . . er . . . attractive.'

It infuriated Tegan to see him talking so calmly about being marooned. 'We could be stuck here forever,' she said. 'Considering the state of the TARDIS.'

'TARDIS?' said the Gravis. 'You have a TARDIS!' Tegan sensed a note of sharp interest in the mechanical croak, and she fancied the pendulum quickened its pace. 'Not any more,' she replied defiantly, and then wished she hadn't. She didn't need the swift admonishing glance the Doctor gave her to realise she'd said too much.

The Doctor stepped in hastily. 'Not any more than any other Time Lord, Gravis. Rather less, in fact. Just the one, in my case . . . some Time Lords have three or four. You like travel?'

'Only those who have been isolated for millenia truly appreciate the power of mobility. Yes, I want to see your TARDIS.'

Tegan nearly said that it was tough luck, but the Doctor's

109

grip on her arm was very firm now. He spoke to the leader of the Tractators in a cooing voice. 'Of course, Gravis. I'd be grateful for your opinion. You're a creature of fine judgement, obviously.'

Tegan found this flattering turn of the conversation very unpleasant, but forced herself to listen in silence while the Doctor went on for a while in the same vein. Only when the conversation turned to the mural carvings, and the Doctor bent close to the wall to inspect them, did he have a chance for a hasty, whispered conference with her out of earshot of the little, ticking translating machine. 'We're in grave danger here, Tegan. So please leave this to me.'

'Maybe, but what's the idea of jollying him along?' hissed Tegan. 'He's disgusting.'

'Greedy, too, and responds to flattery. We'll have to work on that.' And then aloud he said, 'Fascinating. Map of the tunnel system, I suppose?'

'Work on it!' exclaimed Tegan, not letting herself be shushed by the Doctor, even though the little machine was hovering closer now. 'It's a matter of principle, Doctor!'

'What is she saying?' said the machine suddenly. The Doctor smiled at it and then at the Gravis. 'Discussing this most interesting tunnel system. My assistant was pointing out it uses the toroidal principle. It's taken a lot of time to get this far with it, I suppose?'

'We have been marooned out here on Frontios for nearly five hundred years, Doctor. As I'm sure the Time Lords already know.'

'There you are, Tegan,' said the Doctor. 'I told you not to take the narrow view. The Gravis and his friends were on this planet long before the Earth colonists. And finders keepers, eh?'

Tegan's jaw dropped. The Doctor sounded completely serious. 'You can't take sides with them! They made the excavating machine.' The Doctor beamed amicably at the Gravis. 'We're having some communication difficulties here,

110

Gravis. My assistant isn't programmed in the ways of the world. Forgive the naivety.'

'Naivety!' exclaimed Tegan. 'I like that.' And all the pent up, confused emotion that had been welling up in her poured out in a torrent of bitter words.

Mr Range came to a halt at the head of the column. Brazen pushed forward from the rear and found him trembling with indecision. 'Come on, Mr Range. I've got five good men depending on you.'

Mr Range wiped his spectacles. 'I think I remember the way . . .'

'I'll need more than guesswork,' said Brazen drily, 'if I am to lead my men into danger.' Mr Range pushed the spectacles back on his nose and replied in a voice that betrayed his irritation, 'You lead then, if you're not happy with my directions.'

'My job, Mr Range,' said Brazen slowly, 'is carrying out what has to be done. I leave the business of directions to wiser heads.' He intended no irony; for Brazen it was the simple truth. But the point was lost on Mr Range, who protested, 'I can't carry responsibility for this whole expedition!'

'You're Chief Science Officer, as you're fond of telling me, Mr Range. "Chief" means "in charge of", "Science", as I understand it, means "knowing" . . . And "Officer" means that the men are looking to you. Sir.'

Mr Range looked from one to the other of the two junctions that still offered no clue about the direction to take. 'Let's rest for a moment.'

'Better for morale if we push on, Mr Range,' Brazen insisted. 'We'll take it slowly.'

Mr. Range wondered at Brazen's idea of leadership. An authoritative figure firmly dictating direction was more important to him than any question of the rightness of the direction. On reflection Mr Range could see that, abhorrent though it might be to a scientist, this idea made some sense. Had Captain Revere's regime been like that?

By now thoroughly confused, Mr Range chose a tunnel at random. Behind him the Orderlies hitched up their back-packs. They had just begun to move on when someone from the rear came forward with a whispered message for Brazen. The Chief Orderly handed his phosphor lamp over to Mr Range and urged him on down the tunnel. All this sudden whispering and activity confused Mr Range even more, and he wanted to go back for Brazen, who for some reason was being left behind without a lamp. But the Orderlies hurried him onward.

Brazen pressed himself back into a niche in the wall, and stood as still as the rock itself. The wavering light at the end of the tunnel grew larger. Brazen waited until the shadowy shape behind the lamp had almost gone past him. And then he moved, grabbing an arm and a hank of hair and forcing the light up into the face.

It was Turlough.

'You're supposed to be with Norna,' Brazen exclaimed. 'You've left her alone!'

'I thought you might need me,' said Turlough. It hadn't been easy plucking up courage to descend into the tunnel system again. But his own indignation was nothing to that of Mr Range when they caught up with the rest of the expedition. 'What about my daughter!' When Brazen insisted that they needed Turlough, the little scientist vibrated with fury. 'I'm going back . . . someone should be with her.'

'Somebody stop him,' said Turlough. 'It's dangerous.'

But Mr Range had already set off back the way they had come, and Brazen merely shrugged his big shoulders. 'Let him be. He's not the man for the job. He belongs with his daughter.' Nothing would persuade Brazen to part with one of his men to accompany Mr Range, and Turlough had no choice but to lead the expedition on into the tunnel system.

*

The Tractator had Tegan piniored against the wall, as if an invisible plate of glass were being pushed against her chest. 'Doctor!' she called out, her voice hoarse now with talking. 'You can't let them do this to me!'

The Doctor turned to Gravis. 'Look here, I'm terribly embarrassed about this. I can't think what can have caused the malfunction. These serving machines are perfectly reliable on Gallifrey. Probably just that it hasn't been tested for subterranean work.'

'The Guard Tractator will restrain it while I show you more of our work here,' said the translating machine, hovering by the Doctor's ear. As the Doctor strolled with the Gravis towards the cave entrance it added, 'Your serving machine is, if I may say so, a very convincing replica of a humanoid life form.'

'You think so?' the Doctor replied with a note of doubt. 'I got it cheap because the walk's not quite right. But when it's working well it's very useful for keeping track of appointments . . . financial planning . . . word-processing . . . that sort of thing.'

Tegan gasped in astonishment at this extraordinary utterance of the Doctor. But there was nothing she could do about it – the Guard Tractator was immobilising her as effectively as if she were clamped to the wall with hoops of steel. She glowered at the Doctor's retreating back, and when he paused to allow the Gravis to pass through the entrance ahead of him, their eyes met.

Tegan stared at the Doctor she thought she knew – the Doctor into whose TARDIS she had accidentally stumbled all those aeons ago, the Doctor she had nursed through his almost fatal regeneration . . . the Doctor who, for all his mumbling absent-mindedness and corkscrew logic, had managed to bring her safely through more perils than she cared to remember. She stared and stared at him, filling that brief moment of eye contact with all the dumbly outraged and uncomprehending staring she could muster.

And from the Doctor in return came a swift, barely perceptible wink.

Norna had continued laying out the food, unaware of the Ret climbing in through the hatch above her head until it was too late. He was already shinning down the rope when she saw the movement out of the corner of her eye. She called out to the Orderlies she hoped were patrolling the corridor outside, and at the same time grabbed the rope and jerked it with all the strength she could muster. The Ret lost his grip and fell flailing to the floor, where he lay still. The other Ret abruptly ducked his head back out of the hatch and slammed it shut.

The footsteps of an Orderly were approaching down the corridor. A moan came from the crumpled immobile figure on the floor. Norna bent down to tend to him, and suddenly found an arm thrown round her neck, and a hand clamped to her mouth. The footsteps stopped at the door as the Ret dragged Norna down out of sight behind a bench.

The face of an Orderly peered in at the door. The room seemed empty: an array of shotguns propped up against the wall, the remains of an experiment on the workbench, the curious TARDIS hat-stand, and a trestle table laid with food. He crossed to the table and helped himself to a handful of bread cubes. Behind the bench Norna tried kicking her feet, but the Ret tightened his grip on her until she could hardly breathe.

The Orderly wandered out, munching on the bread cubes. The Ret kept tight hold of Norna until his footsteps had receded down the corridor, then jumped to his feet and grabbed one of the shotguns. Held at gunpoint there was nothing Norna could do to stop the Ret helping himself to the food on the table.

Above their heads the hatch opened again, and a second figure began to climb down the rope. Norna glanced up and was immediately struck by a curious stealthiness about his descent. The Ret with the shotgun, having filled his mouth and now stuffing every available pocket, was too engrossed in the food to notice the newcomer, and some intuition told Norna not to alert him.

The descending figure swivelled silently on the rope, and as the light fell on his face Norna recognised him. It was Cockerill! Norna's surprise must have been audible, because the Ret at the table swung round with the shotgun. But before he could lift it to fire, Cockerill had leapt from the rope, landing feet first on the looter's chest and sending the gun flying. The two of them collapsed onto the trestle table, and the food went skidding across the research room floor.

The Ret was the first to retrieve the gun. He scrambled to his feet, levelling it at Cockerill. But now other figures were shinning down the rope – more Rets, as Norna recognised from their matted hair and unkept clothing. For a moment it seemed there would be chaos in the research room, but to her astonishment something very different happened.

The first of the new arrivals felled the looter from behind, and before Norna knew what was happening the table was being set upright again and the food gathered up from the floor. It was a disciplined exercise quite unlike anything she had been led to expect from Rets, and they all seemed to take their orders from Cockerill.

'Have you gone over to the Rets?' Norna asked him when order was restored. 'They seem to have come over to my side,' he said with a thin smile. 'And whose side is that?' she asked. He certainly didn't look like Brazen's man any more.

'The side of Frontios,' he said. 'What's left of it. But from now on we do things my way.' As if to indicate to Norna that the conversation was over, Cockerill snapped his fingers at the men behind him. On his orders they collected the guns and formed a line by the door as he cautiously put his head out into the corridor.

When he looked back into the room he saw that one of his

Retrogrades had fallen out of line and was tearing at the food. Cockerill rounded on him. 'Leave it!' he hissed under his breath. 'Time enough for that when we've taken this ship.' He snapped his fingers again, directing his men to stand ready on each side of the door.

'This isn't the way to do it,' Norna pleaded. 'Please, stop him, somebody . . .' But he had already disappeared through the door, taking one of his men with him on a recce of the corridor. Norna turned to the Rets who remained. 'Why is he doing this?'

The lines of Rets stood at ease, cradling the shotguns. Just when she thought no one was going to give her an answer, somebody said, 'We saw it happen.'

'Happen? What did you see?'

It was another Ret who replied. 'The earth began to suck him down, and then returned him.' And a third added, 'Cockerill's our man for saving this planet.'

She wanted to hear more, but at that moment Cockerill returned. 'All clear. Ready?' he asked.

Norna pushed forward. 'No! Wait! You don't understand . . .' If they went out into the corridors with the guns there would be killing, a war between the Colonists of Frontios, when the real peril lay beneath the ground. But before she could begin to tell him about the Tractators he signalled to two of the Rets. 'She makes too much noise. Take care of her.'

One of them cut down a length of rope, and she felt firm hands dragging her backwards towards the trestle table.

The Doctor arrived back at the cavern with the Gravis in time to see the limp figure of Captain Revere being dragged from the excavating machine. The horribly emaciated face told the story immediately, but the Doctor checked his pulse in case there was any hope of life. The translator spoke in his ear. 'Once life functions are extinct the entity is no longer useful as a motive force.'

'Yes, he seems dead enough . . .' said the Doctor. 'If you like that sort of thing.'

'A waste, but we've had the best of him. You can watch us fit the replacement . . .' The translating machine pivoted round, and the hand whipped into a horizontal position. The Doctor's gaze turned in the direction indicated by the dry, driftwood finger. A spherical cage suspended in the middle of the cavern was being drawn towards them.

'Remarkably ingenious, Gravis . . .' said the Doctor amiably. He had recognised the pathetic occupant of the cage at once by his shock of white hair, but for the moment was keeping his feelings to himself. 'I'm certainly looking forward to seeing . . . seeing . . .' The Doctor was patting his coat, looking for something in his pockets. 'My glasses . . . I've left them with the android. Would you mind if I just . . .' With a grave nod to the Gravis and the other Tractators, he hurried back the way he had come.

As he turned into the tunnel that led to the small cave he realised he hadn't been as clever as he thought. The gruesome translator was still hovering at his elbow. It accompanied him back to the cave and positioned itself strategically beside the Guard Tractator at the door.

Tegan was finding it hard to catch her breath. At the sight of the Doctor she tried to speak, but he stopped her with a nod towards the translator. 'Don't say anything, I've brought a friend with me. They've got Plantagenet. He's alive – just.' Then he turned to the Guard Tractator. 'Came to get . . . a pair of . . . glasses. Spectacles, comprendo?' His gestures to indicate a pair of glasses might have amused Tegan if she had been in a more receptive mood.

The Doctor's lowered voice and elaborate gestures drew the translator over towards them. The moment it came close enough to be out of sight of the Guard Tractator he put a hand out and stealthily stilled the ticking pendulum. 'If I'm right about how this works, we're safe for a moment or two.

117

But I've got to get back. Listen – quick. You're an android . . .'

'I certainly am not . . .' said Tegan indignantly.

'Because if they think you're alive,' the Doctor went on, ignoring her protests, 'they may get the idea of adding you to their human Meccano set. That's the plan they have for Plantagenet.'

Tegan saw the Doctor's point immediately. 'I'm an android,' she said.

'And I'm President of the Tractators' Fan Club. I hate deception, but at the moment we've no other weapon. And that Gravis certainly responds to flattery.'

'But this is dangerous, Doctor,' said Tegan, eyeing the Guard Tractator and very much hoping that it didn't understand English.

'We haven't even begun to know how dangerous they are.' The Doctor nodded towards the map on the wall. 'This tunnel system isn't just for transport and accommodation. I've an idea they're up to something of cosmic proportions.' He bent close to her ear. 'Now here's what we're going to do . . .'

He whispered to her for a moment, then set the translating machine's pendulum swinging again, and with a wave to Tegan said to the gruesome device, 'Come on, Horace. We must get back to the Gravis.' But as they turned into the cavern and the Gravis glided towards them, the translator suddenly asked, 'You found your spectacles, Doctor?'

The Doctor stopped in his tracks. In the excitement of the moment he had forgotten all about the hastily concocted excuse. The Doctor dived for his pockets again. 'They're here somewhere. That's the trouble with being a Time Lord. There's so much to remember, and only one small head to put it all in. I think . . . yes . . .' He had actually managed to find a spectacle case in one of the inner recesses of his coat. He waved it triumphantly. 'The eyes have it, Gravis.'

He flipped open the case and put the spectacles on. They were his half frame glasses, occasionally useful for reading when the print was very small, or the book unusually dull. He peered over them at the Gravis. 'A world of difference. Thank you.'

He could sense he had aroused suspicion. 'These devices help your vision?' the creature asked.

'Poly-directrix lenses with circular polarising filters,' said the Doctor with tremendous confidence. 'Reduce spectral reflection as much as seventy-five percent, without any perceptible deterioration of resolution. Gallifreyan technology – like the TARDIS.'

The Tractators had dragged the cage close to the revolting mechanism of the excavator; inside it Plantagenet crouched, strangely immobile. From the glutinous concave surface of the empty driving section, an indentation like the inside of a halved egg-shell, a complex of curled wire-like umbilicals stretched out towards the prisoner, like some huge rock anemone towards its prey.

11

The Price of Rescue

Suddenly the barred door fell open, and Plantagenet floated forward, released from his cage, and now enmeshed in the invisible prison of the Tractators' gravity beams. He seemed in a dream-state. Ignorant of his surroundings, he edged towards the greedy umbilicals.

'Pay attention, Doctor,' said the Gravis. 'We will now demonstrate how the drive mechanism is installed.' But the Doctor had managed to wander forward between Plantagenet and the excavator. 'One moment. Let me just . . . inspect these very interesting linkages . . .' And he bent towards them, as closely as he dared.

As he pretended to inspect the writhing mechanism, the Doctor peered over the lenses of his glasses at the ring of Tractators around him. Experience had taught him that a plan of action was a useful thing to have at a time like this, but the scheme he had whispered to Tegan had not reckoned on there being so very many of them about the place. The circumstances left him only with a plan of inaction, centring around the general idea that the longer he strung things out the more time there would be to think of something useful.

To add to his general discomfort, Plantagenet chose that moment to open his eyes. He stared up with a look of silent accusation that pained the Doctor more than anything the

Tractators'could have done to him. But the charade had to continue. The Doctor turned back to the excavating machine. 'Yes, very efficient,' he purred. 'You certainly know your mechanics, Gravis. And no shortage of spare parts, eh?'

'Not on Frontios,' said the translator, shaking its head in time to the pendulum.

The Doctor heard a strained voice. 'If it weren't for the bombardment . . .' It was Plantagenet, stirred to speech by a burning anger. The Doctor butted in. 'But it is for the bombardment, isn't it, Gravis? No accident, that.'

'The existence of a heavy asteroid belt in the Veruna system was fortuitous,' said the Gravis. 'But the rest, Doctor, has been our gravitational engineering.'

'I guessed as much,' said the Doctor, eyeing Plantagenet and hoping he was taking all this in. 'A useful asteroid belt out there, some additional gravitational beams from down here, and you're knocking them down like ninepins.'

'I curse the chance that brought us to this unhappy planet,' said Plantagenet. The Doctor shook his head. 'Not chance. Eh, Gravis?'

'You're right, Doctor. Our skill steered the ship here.'

Plantagenet tried to move, but the invisible force bound him. 'The Tractators did that!'

'Their gravity beams again. And that's why the colony-ship systems failed *before* the crash,' the Doctor explained. All the Tractators in a well co-ordinated team could easily send out an electro-magnetic pulse strong enough to bring a ship that size to its knees.

Plantagenet shuddered. But he was puzzled that there was no bombardment in the early days of Frontios.

'They gave the colonists ten years to establish themselves on Frontios,' said the Doctor. 'Then they started building their collection.' The collection of human parts to construct their vile machinery. The Doctor was working the conversation towards the crucial point, the purpose of all this unspeakable activity, but here the Gravis intervened. 'Enough talk, Doctor. The linkages are waiting for their connection.'

A force beyond his control moved the Doctor out of the way, and Plantagenet began to float towards the excavator. The thin umbilicals inside the driving cell stiffened and reached out toward the young leader, sinking themselves into the skin of his neck, back and chest with a sucking sound.

The translating machine had gone to close the cage door, and the Doctor took the opportunity of leaning close to Plantagenet, pretending to inspect the grotesque connection. It gave him a chance to whisper, 'I'm here to help you.' Plantagenet made no secret of his incredulity, but the Doctor was insistent. 'You'll have to trust me. When the time comes, do exactly as I say.'

They were interrupted by the Gravis. Summoning the interpreting machine, he said with more than a touch of pride, 'Now let us show you how we smooth our walls, Doctor.'

'I've been puzzling about why you should need such a fine polish,' said the Doctor. 'More of your gravitational engineering, I suspect.'

'You're getting ahead of yourself, Doctor. We will have to know one another much better before I can discuss that stage of our plans.'

But the Doctor knew enough already to guess. The tunnels acted as wave guides, concentrating the gravitational forces. But why, he still wasn't quite sure. The combined force of all those Tractators, concentrated by a sophisticated ring system, would be astronomical . . . And the system was almost completed.

Turlough peeped cautiously over the top of the boulder. Beyond him the ground sloped sharply away, and the tunnel fanned out, forming a ramp into the great cavern. Towards the bottom of the ramp a smaller cave opened off to the side, and inside the entrance Turlough could see a Tractator, standing motionless as if on guard.

He ducked behind the boulder. The Chief Orderly came forward at a fast, crouching pace, signalling to the rest of the expedition to stay back. 'A frontal assault?' Brazen suggested. 'Seems to be the only way,' Turlough agreed. 'But the small cave puzzles me. I think they're keeping prisoners in there.'

Slowly Turlough lifted his head above the boulder again. He was certain this time that there was somebody inside the cave. When he saw the Tractator at the cave entrance turning in his direction he tried to pull his head down again, but as he moved the world seemed to have gone into slow motion. He felt himself slipping forward, over the boulder.

Brazen pulled at his legs. 'Get down.' But Turlough found the Tractator looking directly up at him. Brazen braced himself against the boulder, and a terrible tug of war began. 'No, let go,' Turlough called down to him. 'It's tearing me apart.'

The Tractator began to emit a deep throbbing sound, echoing a warning through the tunnel system. Turlough was dragged further and further over the top of the boulder, and finally kicked himself free from Brazen's grip. The impetus sent him rolling head over heels down the sloping path directly towards the Tractator. But Brazen had already given the signal, and from all sides the Orderlies swept in upon the Tractator. The moment of surprise did not last long, but it was sufficient to drive the creature away from the cave mouth. With the force on him released, Turlough plummeted down into the cave, to arrive bruised but not seriously injured almost at Tegan's feet.

He took her hand, and together they ran from the small cave. 'You idiot!' said Tegan, 'The Doctor had a plan. You've probably ruined it.'

'Just plain "thanks" would have been enough,' said Turlough.

'You don't understand,' Tegan went on. 'The Doctor's in great danger now.'

The Doctor wasn't the only one, thought Turlough. He surveyed the chaos breaking out at the entrance to the cavern, where Tractators were getting the better of two of the Orderlies, closing into a ball around their bodies. 'Where is he, anyway?'

'Follow me,' said Tegan. They grabbed Brazen out of the melee and ran on down the slope into the cavern.

The Tractators grouped around the excavator were hastily completing the connection of Plantagenet. The machine was already chugging ominously, when Brazen, Turlough, Tegan and the remaining Orderlies charged into the attack. The Doctor shouted to them, 'Stay back. There are too many of them.'

But Brazen had already run forward to release Plantagenet. He stopped, awed by the complexity of the linkages. 'How do we get him out of this . . .' he shouted back at the Doctor.

The Gravis was gliding swiftly towards them. 'Theoretically it's highly complex,' said the Doctor. 'But practically . . .' He was expecting the Gravis to unlease his gravitational power in their direction at any minute, but instead he found the translator flying towards him, the pendulum clicking in double time. 'No, Doctor!' it screamed. 'I forbid you to touch the machine.'

But the Doctor was already reaching out towards the linkages. He gathered the gelatinous threads and thick venous tubes in his fists and pulled with all his strength.

Arcs of multi-coloured light showered from the broken linkages, sizzling in a great rainbow towards the Gravis. The creature reeled back, as Brazen lifted the limp body of Plantagenet out of the egg-like driving cavity.

Two Tractators moved to aid the Gravis, who was turning aimlessly this way and that. 'He's only stunned,' observed the Doctor. 'We'll have to work fast.' Not simply because of the Gravis. Deprived of its driver, the excavator's linkages were waving dangerously, probing the space in front of the machine. 'Careful, these things are lethal,' the Doctor warned Brazen as he dragged the young leader clear. He shouted to Tegan and Turlough. 'Come on, you two. We're getting out of here.'

But Turlough remained motionless in front of the excavator. Its linkages were now waving in a frenzy of movement, and the whole whirring machine had begun to pitch and toss like a ship caught in a storm. Turlough stared at the driverless machine that writhed senselessly in front of his fascinated eyes. Turlough was confronting his nightmare, the horror he had been unable to face. Heedless of the shouts of Tegan and the Doctor, he stood his ground unblinkingly while the broken linkages reached out for him and the great, enticing machine advanced. Like living tentacles the linkages began to fasten on the young man.

The Doctor and Brazen had already run forward. But at that moment one of the Tractators tending the Gravis uncoiled, and froze the Doctor in his tracks. Brazen managed to reach Turlough, and began prising him away from the thrashing sinews. By stretching, the Doctor was almost within touching distance of his young companion. 'My hand . . . Quick!' But he could feel the Tractator behind him pulling him backwards. Turlough's fingertips brushed his . . . and then their hands clasped.

Hating the helpless feeling of being without a weapon, Tegan had picked up a boulder, staggering under its weight. The Doctor had a firm grip on Turlough's hand now, and the Tractator's beam was pulling them both backwards. Tegan waited until Turlough was clear of the last of the flailing tendrils, then slammed the boulder into the Tractator's glowing underbelly.

The Doctor shot forward, grabbing Turlough and almost falling over Tegan. 'Brazen! Run!' he shouted.

But it was too late. Brazen was caught. The machine's polishing arms had closed about his body, and the linkages were beginning to enmesh him, weaving about his chest and face like some fast-growing thicket of brambles. Above his head the vicious excavating jaws began to descend.

The Doctor paused, wondering if there was any chance of saving him. But the Gravis was already stirring. 'Get out of here, Doctor,' Brazen roared at him. 'Hurry, while there's still time.' There was no doubt that time had already run out for Brazen. The excavating jaws were fastening around his head. 'It's too late, Doctor! Go! That's an order!'

Those were his last words. The gnashing edges of the cutters ate into the brave Chief Orderly's body as the movements of the machine became wilder and wilder. The Doctor did not linger to see the rest.

Cockerill's Rets had left Norna face down among the food, her hands roped together underneath the table. With her mouth stuffed full of bread cubes and gagged with a torn strip of cloth, they had made sure she wouldn't call out to anybody. But as they had taken command of the corridor outside, help from that direction wasn't at all likely.

They had overlooked the knives on the table, however. By sliding to one side until the table was in danger of toppling off its trestles, she found she could shake one of the knives towards her face. A crack ran down the middle of the table between the two boards that comprised its surface, and by gripping the hilt between her teeth she was able to push the knife into it so that the blade protruded below. She brought her wrists towards the blade and began slowly sawing at the rope.

When Cockerill and his Rets returned to the Research Room, Norna wasn't immediately missed. Cockerill's chief preoccupation was what to do with the Orderlies he'd captured. 'Think yourselves lucky you're alive,' he said to them. 'We need willing hands, not dead bodies, if we're to build a new Frontios. I never wanted to be a second Plantagenet, but it seems there's no choice.'

Norna stepped out from her hiding place behind the bench, holding the knife at the ready. 'We might not need a second Plantagenet!'

Cockerill spun round. 'What do you mean?' Norna unfolded the story of the expedition to save Plantagenet, and when Cockerill remained incredulous, took them to the trapdoor to the excavation area and showed them where the tunnels began.

'It's a trick,' said one of the Rets. 'She wants us down there so she can trap us.' Another Ret suggested the possibility of an ambush. 'There's something down there,' he said. 'Listen.'

Cautiously they all approached the edge of the trapdoor. There was certainly a scrabbling noise from inside the excavation area. Cockerill directed a phosphor lamp into the blackness, and it picked up the outline of a figure emerging from the tunnel. Battered and exhausted, a weary face looked up at them, the eyes blinking without their accustomed glasses. 'Father!' Norna exclaimed.

'No good . . .' whispered Mr Range. 'Tractators everywhere. Frontios is doomed.'

They were running across the cavern, to where Tegan did not know. The Doctor was holding her hand tightly, which was just as well, because the whole huge space seemed to be spinning and shuddering around them. She glimpsed Turlough's red hair, and somewhere beyond him was Plantagenet and one of the Orderlies they had brought with them; all running to escape from the thunderous screeching and thumping as the excavation machine went berserk, smashing into the walls and shaking the solid rock.

They reached a massive pile of stones that formed a steep ascent up to a narrow cave that might have been the mouth of another tunnel. Here they linked hands, and the Doctor went first, steadying their way up to the temporary haven. Only when she was inside did Tegan dare to look back over her shoulder. Below her she saw the cavern filling with clouds of dust. Of the Gravis there was no sign.

She turned to Turlough. 'If you hadn't been so hypnotised by that machine . . .' She broke off, astonished to find a half smile curling his lip. 'The excavator!' he exclaimed. 'I remember everything. Doctor, I must tell you . . .'

'All in good time,' said the Doctor, leading them further into the tunnel. 'We're not safe yet.'

'But I know who they are!' Turlough insisted, and the Doctor could see from the eyes of his companion that the dark ancestral memories had become clear in his mind.

There was something of the same look in Plantagenet's face. 'And I know what they are trying to do,' said the young leader.

The Doctor would have been happy to pursue this interesting conversation, but at that moment the rocks trembled again, and silt cascaded down from the roof. 'Get down!' he shouted.

It happened again; a huge rumbling sound, and a shock wave that shook the whole tunnel, showering down rocks from the roof and walls. And then there was quiet.

The Doctor crept back to the mouth of the tunnel and looked out into the cavern, where the dust was settling like autumn mist. He could see no Tractators, but he knew they would be lurking in the side tunnels, mustering their strength. The twisted wreck of the excavating machine protruded from piles of rock debris, buried in a grave of its own making. The Doctor thought briefly of Brazen, and of the colonists whose corpses had gone to make up the evil device, and uttered very privately within himself a Gallifreyan word that is said in these circumstances.

His thoughts turned to the living. Turlough knew who the Tractators were . . . and Plantagenet knew what they were up to. The next step was to find somewhere safe, and assemble the facts. He was on the point of returning to the others when he heard a familiar ticking sound coming from somewhere below the cave entrance.

A sinuous, desiccated hand pointed up at him, and a pair of white, protruding eyes swivelled in his direction. He heard the voice of the translating machine raised to screaming pitch. 'We have found you, Doctor. You will pay dearly for this disruption to our plans.'

The Doctor sprinted back down the tunnel, shouting to the others. 'Come on. It's time we left.' They ran on, in places having to clamber over heaps of rubble that the recent tremors had dislodged from the roof and walls. It was an uncertain and dangerous journey, but anything was better than trying to patch up diplomatic relations with the Gravis.

The screech of the translating machine pursued them down the tunnel. 'You cannot escape, Doctor. You will see.' The Doctor began to suspect that the Gravis was right. A toroidal tunnel system would be bound to direct them back to the big cavern, where the Tractators would certainly be waiting.

It was Turlough who pointed out the obvious. 'These aren't Tractator tunnels, Doctor. Look.' In the sombre glow of the phosphor lamps the walls showed up as raw rock, untouched by any excavating machine. It was clear that the creatures had been using parts of this larger natural tunnel system as their raw material.

'We need a rest,' said the Doctor, when after many more twists and turns of the tunnel the ranting accusations of the translator had been left far behind. 'We should be safe here for the moment.' He handed one of the remaining phosphor lamps to the Orderly. 'Keep watch at that end, there's a good chap.' And then he returned to Turlough and Plantagenet. 'All right, what do we know about these creatures?'

Plantagenet leant back against the wall. 'The tunnel system is a giant ring. Smooth and mathematically precise.

A form of accelerator to concentrate the gravitational forces.'

'Yes, yes,' said the Doctor. 'But what are they up to?'

'They're building a gravity motor,' said Plantagenet. Tegan jumped in, bristling with questions. 'A motor? Why would they want a motor inside a planet?'

'That's it!' exclaimed Turlough. 'That's what they do to planets. They're going to drive Frontios.'

So that was it! A plan to steer Frontios through the galaxy under the power of gravity, plundering and stealing wherever they went. And breeding, thought the Doctor grimly. Nesting in new planets. Nowhere in the universe would be safe from them.

The Orderly had stationed himself at a bend in the tunnel, a position that commanded a good straight view of the approach in the direction they had come. For a while he had held the phosphor lamp up high to push back the invading shadows as far as possible, but now his hands were beginning to ache with the cold. He put the lamp down on the ground and rubbed his hands together, and then – because his feet were cold too – began to pace up and down.

If Brazen had still been there to command him perhaps he would not have been so careless. But as he did not know what to expect from the Tractators, he was not even aware when it began to happen. In particular he failed to notice the lamp start to inch away down the tunnel as if by its own accord.

One thought gave the Doctor and his friends some consolation. The ring was not complete yet – Plantagenet was certain of that. 'But if their excavating machine is wrecked,' Tegan said excitedly, 'they won't ever be able to finish it.'

'They have several of the machines,' was Plantagenet's grim reply. 'All they need are drivers. And any one of us would do for that.'

Suddenly there was a throttled scream from beyond the

end of the tunnel. Tegan was the first to react, grabbing a lamp and running recklessly off towards the sound. 'It's the Orderly!'

'Too late, Tegan! Come back,' shouted the Doctor. 'They're here.'

She didn't need the Doctor to tell her that. As he called out to her, a pair of Tractators loomed out of the darkness of the tunnel ahead. She turned and ran back towards the Doctor, and saw him stretching out his hand to her. But the faster she ran the slower her movements became.

Then she saw him raise his hand above his head and hurl his phosphor lamp in a twisting arc into the tunnel behind her. There was a blinding flash, and she heard the Doctor shouting, 'Scatter, everybody. It's our only chance.'

Tegan ran with no thought for time or direction. When she could go no further she found herself alone in a small tunnel, where she pressed herself back against the wall and waited, holding her breath in the echoing, bottomless silence.

She seemed, for the moment at least, to be safe, and she allowed herself to breathe again. When at last she dared raise the lamp to take stock of her surroundings, what she saw made her think she must be dreaming. As the circle of light spread across the wall opposite it revealed a smooth round shape embedded in the rough rock.

She ran to it, brushing away the surface dust. It was a TARDIS roundel.

12

Greed Sets the Trap

A quick tour of the tunnel uncovered other similar panels all the way along the walls. 'The TARDIS,' she said under her breath. 'Bits of it, anyway.' She ran along further and found a whole stretch of one wall faced with the same dear familiar design.

Though she was no expert, it seemed to her that the tremendous force exerted by the Tractators had been enough to suck the Doctor's time-machine underground and explode it along the tunnels, embedding its fragments in the rock. Probably the destruction had not been intentional; if the Tractators did not know that the police box was a TARDIS – and there was no reason why they should – its peculiar time physics would almost certainly have led them to underestimate its mass as an object in space.

Further along the extraordinary hybrid tunnel she found herself surrounded by raw rock again. In a way that was better than being confronted with a mocking reminder of the TARDIS. Nevertheless, she determined to remember the way back, so that when the Doctor turned up again she would be able to show him the panels. There was the remotest possibility that he might be able to do something about it.

The mood of optimism in which she pushed on along the tunnel did not prepare her for what she found when she came to the next bend. There were three of them, coming from the opposite direction, their pallid, pulsating under-bellies forming a wall of glowing whiteness in the darkness ahead.

She turned and ran back the way she came. Raw rock and TARDIS panels flashed by her. At first she made good speed, but the Tractators had been alerted and it wasn't long before she felt that sickening oiliness dragging at her limbs. The rock and the panels slowed, like a film running down.

She took an abrupt turn to the left, down a passage that was little more than a crevice in the rock. She was hoping it would be too narrow for the Tractators to follow, but it quickly broadened out into a corridor so densely packed with the roundel-inscribed panels that for a moment it was almost like being back in the TARDIS itself.

Until she found the corridor blocked by a wall of sheer rock. It was a dead end, and there was no way to go but back the way she had come. But she could hear the Tractators advancing from that direction, and feel the suction of their gravitational pull on her body.

She heard a ticking noise. To her horror the translating machine appeared around the corner in front of her. She was being pulled towards it, dragged along the wall of the corridor. Her hands scrabbled for a hold, anything to prevent her being sucked towards the loathsome device.

Behind the machine loomed the great scaly body of the Gravis. The ticking machine spoke his thoughts. 'So this is the "android". But perhaps I have been deceived. I think we have found our new driver.'

Now there were two more Tractators behind him, and the pull on her body was almost unbearable. She clung tightly to some small, jutting object protruding from the wall behind her – only that saved her from being whisked down the corridor.

As the Tractators bore down on her it occurred to her to

wonder what manner of thing it was that offered itself so conveniently as a hand hold. It was hand-shaped, and at hand-height. Objects like this did not occur by accident.

It was a handle. A door handle. And where there was a door handle, thought Tegan, her mind racing, and the creatures almost within touching distance, the odds on finding a door were very, very promising. She turned the handle and, pushing backwards with a mighty jump, tumbled through the space that opened up behind her.

She threw her weight against the door, slamming it shut, and then leant back to take a deep breath. It was only then that she saw the very last thing she expected – the Doctor throwing switches on the console.

'Glad you could join us,' said the Doctor. 'Turlough and Plantagenet and I have been working out a plan of action.'

It wasn't the whole console room, but there was certainly enough of it to be recognisable. The circular space in which she had spent so much time during her travels with the Doctor was almost complete in places, and if you ignored the large sections of wall that were only dark, bare rock, it was almost like being in the TARDIS again.

'Well, whatever this plan is,' said Tegan. 'It had better work. They're right outside!'

'I hoped they might be,' the Doctor replied carelessly. He turned his attention back to activating the banks of switches on the console. That was what made it feel so much like the TARDIS, Tegan realised with a jolt. The lights on the array of panels that formed the centre of the room were flashing, almost as if they were in flight.

'I've remembered the secret of the Tractators,' Turlough explained. 'They're not really dangerous!'

'They certainly fooled me,' said Tegan without a smile.

Plantagenet's eyes glittered with the light of renewed hope. 'It's the Gravis they draw their strength from. The Gravis is the key. Turlough says that without him all these Tractators are just harmless burrowing earth-dwellers.'

'A sort of queen bee,' said Tegan. 'So all we've got to do is find a way of isolating him from the others. That's going to be fun.' She looked across to the console. The Doctor had switched on so many lights, dials, panels, screens and enunciators that now it was all lit up like a Christmas tree. 'What on earth is he doing?' she asked Turlough. 'He's not trying to take off, surely?'

'Unfortunately not. None of the controls is functional.'

Tegan wanted to know what possible value there could be in throwing switches, closing circuits, activating activators and generally going through the motions of powering up the TARDIS when there was no TARDIS and no power. Turlough and Plantagenet were on the point of explaining when the Doctor stepped back from his elaborate endeavours and, clapping his hands with a note of finality, said, 'Good, we're ready. This will either solve this whole Tractator problem – and repair the TARDIS at the same time . . .' He tailed off, looking over the console as if giving it a last minute check. 'Or?' prompted Tegan.

'Or it won't,' the Doctor replied crisply, heading for the door through which Tegan had so abruptly entered, a door that in the normal way of things would be expected to lead to the TARDIS corridors. 'Now I suggest you all get under cover.'

Outside the Gravis and the other Tractators were surrounding the door. The translator hovering at the side of the Gravis barked, 'It is useless to hide. We have you completely in our control now.'

The Doctor peeped out into the tunnel and said mildly, 'Quite. I'd like to negotiate a surrender.'

'There is nothing to negotiate,' said the Gravis, speaking through the machine.

The Doctor nodded amiably. 'I agree. You can have it all. Frontios, its unhappy occupants, the lot. I don't think it's fair for us Time Lords to interfere. Why should we let a bunch of stuffed shirts on Gallifrey deprive you of your own transportation?' The Doctor beamed at the Gravis, and then added slyly, '. . . however primitive.'

'Primitive?' echoed the machine.

The Doctor smiled unassumingly. 'In comparison to Gallifreyan time technology, of course. But what isn't?' And he chose that moment to let go of the door handle, allowing the door to swing open behind him. This act of apparent negligence gave the Gravis his first tantalising glimpse of the glittering lights of the console.

The pulse of the translator's pendulum quickened. 'The TARDIS!' it said. 'You have the TARDIS here.'

The Doctor looked casually over his shoulder. 'What, this? Ah, yes . . .' He pulled the door shut again and reverted to the negotiations. 'As I say, Gravis . . . you hold onto Frontios and all the fixtures and fittings appertaining thereunto, and I'll pull my Tardis together and get off your patch.'

'I should like to see it, this TARDIS,' said the Gravis. The Doctor scratched his head. 'Well, I don't mean to be difficult, but it's not all here at the moment. It's spatially distributed to optimise the . . . er . . . packing efficiency of the real-time envelope.' And at the same time, quite accidentally, he let go of the door handle again. The Gravis and his translating machine pushed forward towards the door, drawn by the promise of the twinkling console. 'No, I really wouldn't,' protested the Doctor. 'Believe me, you're not seeing it at its best . . .'

But there was no stopping the creature. The winking lights, with their promise of time-travel technology, attracted him with a force far stronger than his own gravitational beams. It was greed that drew the Gravis into the Doctor's picturesque trap.

The creature approached the console, the translator hovering at his side. 'The power of travel is beautiful, Doctor. Very beautiful.'

'I would just beg you not to touch the instrumentation,

Gravis,' fussed the Doctor. 'Well, not that you, of course – touch. But do be careful not to move anything. This particularly . . .'

The Gravis sent the translator whirling towards the lever the Doctor was indicating, and the sinewy hand snatched at it. As the lever moved, a panel in the wall slid open, revealing a glowing patch of colour that swam into focus until it became a picture of the surrounding tunnels.

'Oh dear,' said the Doctor. 'Now you've activated the viewer screen. The auto-scan circuitry is picking up the location of all the concealed TARDIS components.' He smiled. 'Nothing is hidden from you, eh, Gravis? Though I don't suppose it's within even your powers to reassemble them. In any case, what would you want with a de-luxe intergalactic Time and Relative Dimension in Space machine . . . ?'

But the Gravis was now trembling with interest, and the translator's pendulum was clicking like a Geiger counter. 'I do want it, Doctor. A TARDIS. Infinite travel within my grasp!'

'I beg you, Gravis. Take everything else, but leave me the TARDIS.' But the Doctor's nicely calculated display of distress only seemed to urge the Gravis on. The creature's scaly body began to uncurl like some grotesque flower blossoming as he concentrated his will on the tunnels. 'No, please, Gravis. Spare me the TARDIS.'

'I will have it!' came the triumphant reply. Turlough's head appeared above the console. 'What's he doing now, Doctor?' The Doctor pushed him down out of sight again with a whispered 'Sssh. This is not the time to disturb his concentration.'

They felt the floor under their feet begin to tremble, and the lights on the instrument panel flickered and dimmed . . . A rushing wind swept around the room, and everything seemed to go into a spin, shaking out the Doctor's companions from their hiding place beneath the console.

'Doctor! He's destroying us!' cried Tegan. 'What have you done?'

'Brace yourselves!' came the Doctor's succinct reply, in a firm voice intended to dismiss any sentimental nonsense about destruction – although in the heart of his two hearts he wasn't so sure.

As the Gravis opened himself out to his full extent, swaying his body like a tree in a gale, the wind swelled, and the vibration increased until the whole room seemed to be screaming about their ears.

Norna was tending her father's cuts and bruises when the shock wave reached the research room. The trestle table shuddered, tipping plates and cutlery onto the floor, and on the work bench the glass retorts chattered against each other so violently that one of them shattered. 'The end!' exclaimed Mr Range. 'The end of Frontios!'

Norna put her cool hand on her father's forehead. It was frightening not to know what was happening down there. But she wasn't inclined to despair. Not yet. 'It might be the beginning, Father,' she said.

Cockerill was rounding up the last of the dissenting Orderlies. At the first tremor his men stood still, frightened, not knowing what to expect next. He went down on his knees and put his ear to the ground, and heard the deep trembling notes rolling away like retreating thunder. The sounds came again and again, bringing a handful of Rets, seeking safety in numbers, running from the sand dunes into the settlement to swell the small band that had already joined Cockerill. Then more followed, and soon myriad voices were asking each other what was happening. The huge, whispered question was brought at last to Cockerill.

Cockerill's voice was clear and confident, a tone that would have met with Brazen's approval. 'The cause of this new phenomenon is not known at this time,' he announced to the crowd gathered in the open space outside the medical shelter. 'I believe there is no danger, as long as we stay together. You will be kept informed of any developments.'

Deep below ground, the shell of the TARDIS console room was vibrating so wildly that it seemed to its occupants that its very molecules were bound to fly apart. In the centre of it all, reared up on his hind quarters, his underbelly emanating a pale, undulating light, the Gravis had swollen almost to bursting point with concentration on his task.

Tegan, Turlough, Plantagenet and the Doctor clung to the console as if it were a life raft on a tempestuous sea . . . but they survived. The translating machine was not so lucky. Its pendulum was the first component to be shaken off, and thereafter the cadaverous fingers lost their grip on the console, and the whole device was thrown about the room, battered from wall to wall, eventually to fall to the floor as a useless heap of gristle and wire.

'The TARDIS can't stand this, Doctor!' shouted Tegan.

'It's kill or cure,' said the Doctor. 'Look!' And he pointed to the viewer screen, where a succession of images tumbled one upon the other like autumn leaves swept up in a gale. They saw surfaces of dust blasted away to reveal the white roundels of the TARDIS walls. They saw a door embedded in the raw rock fly open, and the room within turn inside out before their eyes. They saw whole corridors tugged away from the rock by some unseen force. A roundel went rolling away down the tunnel. Panels joined, and suddenly became illuminated. And they saw glimpses of the Tractators dispersing down the tunnel system like mice frightened by a vacuum cleaner.

'The TARDIS is coming together!' Tegan exclaimed.

'But surely that's impossible,' Turlough shouted over the noise.

139

'For you and me maybe,' came the Doctor's reply. 'But when the Gravis really wants something . . .'

Tegan held her breath. At last the TARDIS was going to be repaired. Better than that, if she understood Turlough's explanation of the Doctor's plan correctly, at any moment now the plasmic outer walls would seal . . . closing off the inner dimensions of the TARDIS.

'If your calculations are correct, Turlough,' the Doctor shouted, 'the vital link between the Gravis and his Tractator chums will switch off. . . . just like that.' He snapped his fingers, although the sound was lost in the rush of wind. 'Any minute now . . . Hold on!!!'

They heard it clearly above the tumult; a loudly echoing thud, like the sound of submarines colliding. The lights flickered . . . and then brightened, showing a console room that was whole again, the patches of bare rock replaced by the familiar white walls.

In the vast vacuum of silence that followed, the Gravis teetered on his rear legs and began to collapse. The effort of drawing the monumental mass of the TARDIS together had almost drained him of his powers, and now the dimensional isolation completed the task. Tegan felt rather sorry for the creature. As it rolled into a large silver ball, its closely-packed scales resembling exotic inscriptions, it began to look less and less like the evil hunger beneath the earth, and more and more like a slightly obscure archaeological find in some neglected corner of a South Kensington museum.

Plantagenet was the first to speak. 'Is he dead, Doctor?'

'No. But quite harmless. And as long as we keep him isolated from the dimensions of Frontios he'll stay that way.'

'But we can't go dragging around the universe with a dormant Gravis under the console,' said Tegan. The Doctor was notoriously weak on practicalities.

'As long as there are no other Tractators around he can't

140

do any harm,' the Doctor said. 'And vice versa. The first thing we'll do with the TARDIS is drop him off on some remote planet.'

Sunlight was streaming down on the little settlement from a sky so clear and blue that Mr Range, shading his eyes and peering up into it through his steel-rimmed glasses, almost fancied he could see the Doctor's TARDIS. A nonsensical thought, he realised, for it was probably still a million or so miles away.

He returned to his supposed supervision of the team of repatriated Rets repairing the medical shelter door. His own role was hardly necessary as he knew very little about doors, and the workers were so willing that they needed no encouragement from him. Cockerill had given him the job as a chance to recover from his experience below ground, and the cuts and bruises and stiffness of the limbs were healing nicely in the sunshine.

The workers were on the point of restoring the door to its hinges, when there was a sudden flurry and whispering and bowing of heads. Plantagenet stepped out through the doorway. He was dressed in formal garments that made him look almost sturdy, though his face still bore the marks of his recent adversity. Behind him, also in formal attire and looking every inch the professional, came Cockerill.

They both looked up into the sky. 'A brave man, this Doctor,' said Plantagenet, 'travelling with the Gravis on board.'

'It's quite harmless now,' said Mr Range. 'I inspected the creature myself.'

They stayed to watch the door being replaced on its hinges, and then, taking Mr Range with them in his role of technical adviser, made a brief survey of the settlement, discussing the best strategy for phasing the repairs. Now that most of the Rets had returned from the sand dunes, manpower was in plentiful supply. Mr Range was even bold enough to sketch a scenario for completing the first stage of the Long Path back to knowledge.

At the colony-ship entrance they ran into Turlough and Norna, carrying the Doctor's hat-stand. The Doctor was due back at about this time, but Turlough knew the TARDIS and its casual observance of the niceties of mere physical time and space, and warned them not to expect miracles.

'But we're used to miracles from the Doctor,' said Plantagenet, as they walked back to the medical shelter. 'After all, he gave us our freedom.'

Cockerill nodded. 'No more terror descending from the sky. . . .'

He was interrupted by a whirring, chuffing sound that seemed to come from above their heads. There was a general movement, and signs of panic among the Rets. Turlough laughed. 'If you don't count the TARDIS!'

Several cubic feet of air in front of the medical shelter took on a bluish hue, and solidified into the familiar shape of the police box. Almost immediately the door was flung open and the Doctor stepped briskly out, inordinately pleased with himself at having returned on time.

'Well, that's that,' he grinned. 'The Gravis is safe on the uninhabited planet of Kolkokron exercising his animal magnetism on the rocks and boulders.'

Tegan slipped out behind him. 'It's nothing but rocks and boulders out there. All the planets are deserted, according to the TARDIS scanners.'

'Better than being among enemies, as we thought,' Cockerill observed. And a moment of silence followed as they absorbed the implications. Plantagenet put it into words. 'So the last of Mankind is, after all, quite alone.'

'Alone, but in good hands,' said the Doctor, looking at Plantagenet and Cockerill. 'Speaking of which . . .' He beckoned to Turlough and Norna to bring the hat-stand over, and continued, with a hint of embarrassment, 'I thought . . . some sort of memento to mark the occasion. It's not much, I know. A farewell token.'

'Frontios is honoured, Doctor,' said Plantagenet. 'But surely you'll stay a little longer to enjoy the new colony we're building.'

The Doctor sighed like the busy man he was. 'Too much repair work of my own to be done. The stabilisers need realigning, and the secondary drive system will have to be completely reprogrammed. . . . And as for the Architectural Configuration – weeks of work putting that right, I'm afraid. We really must be going.'

'You can do that here on Frontios,' Plantagenet suggested.

The Doctor opened the TARDIS door. 'Time and the Time Laws don't permit, I'm afraid. There's an etiquette about these things, which we've rather overlooked.'

Mr Range ran forward. 'But Doctor, you've done so much for us already.'

'Quite,' said the Doctor. 'Don't mention it.' And with that he disappeared into the TARDIS interior. Plantagenet turned to Tegan and Turlough, who were preparing to follow him. 'Are you sure we can't press him to stay?'

'After all he's done . . .' urged Norna, 'he just says "don't mention it"!'

'I think he means it literally,' said Turlough, shaking her hand and disappearing inside the TARDIS almost as abruptly as the Doctor.

'That's right,' Tegan added. 'Don't mention it – to anybody. If the Time Lords find out there'll be serious trouble!'

And with that Tegan stepped through the blue door. A moment later the TARDIS was gone, leaving Frontios to a more hopeful fate. Plantagenet and the Colonists of Frontios kept the secret of the Doctor's dubious intervention, and the Time Lords never got to hear of it.

More serious trouble was on the way for the Doctor nevertheless. But that was only to be expected.